W9-BON-438

Game Plan

By the same author

Backfield Package

Forward Pass

Halfback Tough

Outside Shooter

Point Spread

Quarterback Walk-on

Rebound Caper

The Rookie Arrives

Running Scared

Soccer Duel

Tournament Upstart

Wilderness Peril

Winning Kicker

Game Plan

Thomas J. Dygard

Morrow Junior Books
NEW YORK

Dedicated to
Adam Nathaniel Stevens

Printed in the United States of America.

1 2 3 4 5 6 7 8 9 10

Library of Congress Cataloging-in-Publication Data

Dygard, Thomas J.
Game plan / by Thomas J. Dygard.
    p.   cm.
Summary: When the Barton High football coach's hospitalization
forces skinny student manager Beano Hatton to take over coaching
the team, he must deal with a rebellious quarterback and his own
lack of confidence.
ISBN 0-688-12007-5
[1. Football—Fiction.   2. High schools—Fiction.   3. Schools—
Fiction.]   I. Title.
PZ7.D9893Gam   1993
[Fic]—dc20   92-47252   CIP   AC

Chapter 1

It was amazing, really, the transformation of Beano Hatton from student manager to head coach of the Barton High football team in the course of one day.

The players, accustomed to seeing Beano passing out gear in the dressing room and delivering the water bottles on the practice field, could not believe it. As student manager, Beano was in charge of fetching, delivering, and collecting anything needed by anyone on the football team. But directing the team?

Others in the student body at Barton High knew the skinny, bespectacled Beano Hatton as a confident, scholarly student who always got straight As. But football coach? Beano?

Around town, fans of the Barton High Tigers

reacted to the stunning news in a variety of ways. Mr. Barber, who ran Barber's Drug Store, broke out laughing and announced, "This is something I've got to see." He promptly left the drug store in the hands of Mrs. Winfield, who sold cosmetics and worked the cash register, and headed for the practice field. At the sheriff's office, Chief Deputy Frank Albright's mouth dropped open and he was, for the first time in anyone's memory, left speechless. Aaron Warren, the elderly owner and publisher of the Barton *Chronicle*, was never left speechless. He announced that "those people at Barton High have lost their minds." His nephew John Bagley, who was the sole full-time editorial employee of the *Chronicle*, mentioned that he might write an editorial reflecting his uncle's opinion.

Two people seemed neither surprised nor troubled by the startling news racing around town.

One was Walton Custer, who taught American History at Barton High. He met each question, each exclamation with a knowing look and a smile and the same comment: "Beano is a smart young man. He's capable of doing almost anything he sets his mind to do, and that probably includes coaching the Tigers."

The other person who did not show any signs

of being surprised or troubled—at least outwardly—was Beano Hatton.

* * *

It all began the previous Friday night, after the Tigers had defeated Wolfton High in their next-to-last game of the season.

All that remained on the schedule was the game against the Bobcats from Carterville, a town twenty miles west of Barton. The Bobcats were Barton High's fiercest rival in the league of tiny high schools in northeast Indiana. A victory over Carterville would make the season a success. A loss would be bitter medicine, with the taste lingering through the winter.

Following their victory over Wolfton High, the Tigers were shouting and cheering and laughing their way through their showers in the dressing room, while Beano collected the soiled uniforms and packed away the footballs.

Coach Henry Pritchard was as happy as the players and was laughing and shouting with them. The next morning would be time enough to begin worrying about the upcoming Carterville Bobcats game. This was the moment for celebration, and he was enjoying himself.

The players, now in their street clothes, left the

dressing room in groups of two, three, and four.

Finally, as always, only Coach Pritchard and Beano remained.

"See you Monday, Coach," Beano said, and headed for the door and the eight-block walk home.

"Right, Beano," Coach Pritchard said.

A short time later, maybe only fifteen or twenty minutes, Coach Pritchard drove slowly into the intersection of Hays and Dustin streets, and a speeding pickup truck running through a stop sign smashed into the passenger side of his car.

In the emergency room at Barton Memorial Hospital, the medical team pronounced Coach Pritchard to be in critical condition with numerous serious injuries, and placed him in the intensive-care ward.

The police called Coach Pritchard's wife, who had gone home with a neighbor right after the game, and then called the principal of Barton High, Edward Tyler. Both of them rushed to the hospital.

Early the next morning, Principal Tyler convened a faculty meeting to consider what the Tigers were going to do without their coach.

Barton High, a small school, had one football coach—Henry Pritchard, who also taught biology. There was no assistant football coach to step in. Yet there was a football game coming up, and the first day of practice for that game—Monday—was only two days away.

Some of the faculty members suggested canceling the game. How could the Tigers practice and play without a coach? And if they did manage to practice and play the game without a coach, weren't they risking a humiliating defeat? Better to cancel the game, they said.

"Not if I can help it," Principal Tyler said. "Football is an activity at Barton High, same as any other activity—the school paper, the senior play— and if there is any way possible for us to carry this activity to its normal conclusion, I want us to do it. The boys have worked hard all season, and we owe it to them—if we can deliver it."

The room was silent as no one spoke aloud the question in all their minds: Who would coach the team through the practice week and in the game?

For a moment all eyes fell on Barton High's two basketball coaches, Jim Beardsley of the boys' team and Brenda Wyandotte of the girls' team.

"No way," Coach Beardsley said. "The basketball team has already played three games. I can't coach both football and basketball at the same time, plus carry the load of the phys-ed classes."

Nobody argued. For one thing, at Barton High

basketball was top priority among the sports, football second priority.

Coach Wyandotte could have said the same thing, but instead she simply smiled and said, "I don't think it would work in any case." Nobody argued with her, either.

After a moment of hopeless silence, Principal Tyler produced a faculty list. Aside from himself, Coach Pritchard, and Coach Beardsley, there were only three men on the list. None of them had the least bit of experience with football.

"Maybe the captains could do it—Marty Tucker running the offense and Larry Slider handling the defense," somebody suggested.

Principal Tyler thought of Marty Tucker, the quarterback, and linebacker Larry Slider, and wrinkled his brow. Marty was a prima donna who loved the starring role on the football team. Left to his own devices, he was sure to pass or run himself on every down. Marty needed direction. Larry was a prima donna too, but of a different sort. He was quite strong, and very proud of it. Beyond that, it was difficult to imagine Larry Slider in a leadership role.

Finally Principal Tyler said, "No, we're talking about organizing a practice week, for one thing. And in a game, *one* person has to make the decisions for the team. We can't have the two of them arguing about whether to punt or go for it on fourth down."

Mr. Custer came up with what everyone seemed to think was a good suggestion. "We've got some former football players living in Barton. They're not experienced as coaches, but at least they've played the game," he said.

With an air of relief, everyone accepted the suggestion and the meeting broke up, leaving Principal Tyler to dial former players on the telephone.

No, Jerry Burton couldn't do it. The quarterback of the Tigers twelve years ago was now a salesman working on commission. He could not afford to take off a solid week of afternoons to conduct the practice sessions, especially on such short notice. He was very sorry. He would have liked to help, but he couldn't.

Luke Taylor, a tackle on the Barton High team fourteen years ago, liked the idea but was scheduled to attend a convention in Chicago over the weekend. He was going to be leaving town on Thursday. Coaching the Tigers was out of the question.

Principal Tyler kept placing calls. Sometimes he heard another good reason why it was impossible to meet his request. Sometimes he left a message, which only served to delay yet another good reason why taking over as emergency coach was out of the question.

He made and received calls through lunch, and at the finish he had eight rejections. All of them had good reasons and all expressed a desire to help—but they couldn't.

Principal Tyler sat at his desk for several minutes after the final conversation, staring through the light cast by his lamp into the gray gloom of the November afternoon.

He could take on the job himself, he thought. Maybe he would have to. He knew little about football, but surely he could get the team through the practice week and, somehow, through the game with the Carterville Bobcats. But Principal Tyler carried a heavy load of duties at tiny Barton High, and there was an important school-board meeting on Thursday that required preparation as well as his attendance.

He toyed with the idea of calling Norton State College, just forty miles away, and asking if someone—maybe an assistant coach or a senior player—might be interested and available. But no, Norton State had its own game to play this weekend. Besides, Principal Tyler did not have any money in the tight Barton High budget to pay an emergency football coach.

Finally he heaved a sigh, reached across and turned off his desk lamp, stood up and put on his coat, and walked out of his office, resigned to having to cancel the game.

That night, at home, Principal Tyler received a telephone call from Walton Custer. The history teacher wanted to know if Principal Tyler had had any luck in his search. Principal Tyler told Mr. Custer that he had drawn zeroes with every call. It looked as if they would have to cancel the game.

"But, Ed, you'd rather not cancel the game, isn't that right?" Mr. Custer asked.

"Of course."

"In that case," Mr. Custer said, "I have an idea."

Beano Hatton was puzzled by the summons to Principal Tyler's office during first-period physics on Monday morning. Troublemakers were told to report to the principal's office. And Beano Hatton was not a troublemaker.

Walking along with Margaret Young, the student clerk who had delivered the message, Beano thought it might have something to do with Coach Pritchard's injury—by now he and everyone else at Barton High knew about it. And more than anyone else at school, Beano had to be told what was going to happen. After all, he was the student manager of the team.

Entering Principal Tyler's office, Beano saw Mr. Custer seated on the sofa. The teacher smiled at him.

Principal Tyler was seated behind his desk, wearing a look on his face of—well, there was no other word for it—disbelief at what he was about to say.

Beano nodded a greeting, and the principal said, "Have a seat, Beano."

Beano sat in a chair angled in front of the desk, facing both Principal Tyler and Mr. Custer.

"You know of Coach Pritchard's accident, of course," Principal Tyler said.

"Yes."

Principal Tyler took a deep breath, and the look of disbelief on his face deepened.

"We obviously have to make emergency arrangements for the football team for the Carterville game," he said.

Beano nodded.

"We've been working on —investigating—various possible courses of action all weekend."

Beano waited.

Another deep breath. Then Principal Tyler said,

"We'd like for you to take over the direction of the team this week, for this last game."

Beano stared at Principal Tyler through his glasses without changing expression. Then he said, "All right."

Principal Tyler frowned. He appeared taken aback. Then he said, "That's all—just 'All right'?"

"I know I can do it," Beano said.

Still frowning, Principal Tyler spoke slowly. "I believe you can," he said.

Chapter 2

Beano walked halfway down the empty corridor, past a couple of classrooms full of students, and stopped. He turned and waited until Mr. Custer emerged from Principal Tyler's office. Then he hailed him.

Approaching, Mr. Custer said, "Yes, Beano?"

"Can I talk to you?"

Mr. Custer watched Beano a moment. He was probably thinking of a place where they could talk, since teachers at Barton High did not have private offices. Principal Tyler's office offered the only real privacy, unless a vacant classroom could be found. Then Mr. Custer said, "Certainly, Beano. Let's go to the cafeteria. Mrs. Mulholland's crew will be beginning the preparations for lunch, but we ought to be able to find a table where we can sit."

They walked together the rest of the way along

the corridor, then down a short flight of stairs to the same level as the gymnasium, turned right, and pushed their way through swinging doors into the cafeteria.

Mrs. Mulholland and three other women were working at the steam tables at the far end of the cafeteria.

Mr. Custer gestured toward a table near the swinging doors, and he and Beano sat down facing each other.

"What is it, Beano?"

"I'm scared."

The surprise showed on Mr. Custer's face. "You didn't seem scared when Principal Tyler put the proposition to you in his office just now."

Beano, who never had trouble thinking, explained what went through his mind when Principal Tyler made his proposal. "If I was going to say yes, I had to appear confident in order to gain Principal Tyler's confidence. And I thought I did have to say yes."

Mr. Custer nodded the same way he did when Beano was answering a question in his American History class.

"After all, who else was there to do it?" Beano asked by way of explaining why he felt he had to say yes.

"Frankly, nobody," Mr. Custer said.

"Yes," Beano said softly, looking past Mr. Custer at a spot on the wall. "But I'm scared that I can't do it. I had the feeling the minute I walked out of Principal Tyler's office." He paused and looked at Mr. Custer. "I've never had that feeling before."

Mr. Custer waited a moment before speaking. Then he said, "Beano, your feelings are natural, quite normal. You've taken on an immense challenge—like a man—and you'll meet the challenge like a man."

Beano frowned. Mr. Custer was talking to him like his father used to do before Beano finally told him to cut it out, that he would try to do his best and that was all he could do. He looked up at Mr. Custer and said, "But—"

Mr. Custer raised a hand a couple of inches off the table and interrupted Beano. "Let me finish," he said.

Beano nodded without speaking.

"As I said, your doubts about yourself are normal. And I'll add that there will be others who will have their doubts too, and they may speak out about their doubts. But Beano, history is full of men who took on great tasks with great self-doubt about their ability to carry through on them—and they had to fight off the doubters around them, too. But they succeeded in the end."

Beano gave a little sigh and waited for Mr. Custer to finish. Clearly, the teacher did not understand.

"Harry Truman was one. When President Roosevelt died and Truman became president, there were a lot of critics who called him a pip-squeak and said he wasn't capable of being president. There were plenty of doubters around, and he may have had some doubts of his own, although he never acted like it. What he acted like was—well, he acted like he was the boss, because he was, in fact, the boss. And he turned out to be a very successful president."

Beano frowned. This wasn't helping much.

"There are two points in there for you to consider, Beano."

"Oh?"

"One, Harry Truman was better suited by experience and temperament to take over as president than anyone—possibly himself included—realized at the time. And you, Beano, are better equipped to coach the Tigers than you or anyone else might realize."

Beano waited.

"Coach Pritchard was telling me after the last

faculty meeting about the plays you devised for the Tigers. He said that you'd seen them in a pro game on television and realized they could be adapted to the Tigers' players. He said you had what he called 'a good football mind.' In short, you know what you're doing, better than you realize."

"Maybe. But—"

"And," Walton Custer continued, "when Principal Tyler tells the team this afternoon that you are the coach now and for the Carterville High game, you will be the coach—the boss—and if you act like the coach and boss, you won't have any trouble."

He leaned back and watched Beano.

Beano tilted his head slightly. He understood Mr. Custer's points. He did feel he knew football, same as he knew his classroom subjects. And he decided that he liked Mr. Custer's point that, with Principal Tyler's announcement, Beano did become the coach. At that moment, the players— Marty Tucker, Larry Slider, the others—needed his approval, not the other way around.

Beano smiled at Mr. Custer. "I understand and I agree. Thank you."

Mr. Custer returned Beano's smile and began to get to his feet.

Beano shoved back his chair and stood up.

Together, without speaking, they walked toward the swinging doors leading out of the cafeteria.

But, Beano thought as they walked, all of this is easier said than done.

All through the day, questions zoomed through the corridors of Barton High and whirled around in the classrooms.

Was Barton High going to cancel the Carterville game? The Tigers had no coach, so how could they practice? Where would they get a game plan? Who would direct the team from the sidelines during the game?

Then there was the recurring rumor that an emergency coach had been found to step in.

Remarkably, these rumors were following the same pattern as the faculty discussion in Principal Tyler's office on Saturday morning. First, there were rumors that a faculty member was going to take over. Who? Mr. Custer? What did he know about football? Nothing. He talked about Washington crossing the Delaware. What did that have to do with football?

Well then, who? Maybe Coach Beardsley. No,

that was impossible, with basketball season already underway. How about Coach Wyandotte? That brought some jokes about a woman giving a halftime talk in a dressing room full of boys. But jokes aside, the girls' basketball season was also underway.

Or maybe an assistant coach from Norton State would be released for the week. Although he wouldn't know anything about the Barton High players and their style of football, he would have the practice week to learn. But Norton State had its own game to play this weekend.

And yes, there were men living in Barton who had played for the Tigers. They knew football from their playing days. And they regularly attended the Tigers' games, so they would be familiar with the players and the style of football. Sure, one of them could do the job.

Then somebody reported that he had heard that Jerry Burton had been approached by Principal Tyler and that he couldn't possibly give up the time from his job. Well, maybe another one of the former players.

In the swirl of rumors, Beano Hatton's name never came up. Beano listened without comment to the corridor chatter between classes and during lunch period. He nodded thoughtfully, shoving his glasses back up on his nose, and said nothing.

He did not say anything either when the rumor began circulating that an arrangement had indeed been made and that Principal Tyler would announce it to the team in the dressing room before practice.

But Beano did tell one person. It was an administrative necessity, he figured. With Beano as coach, the Tigers no longer had a student manager. They needed one. Beano's choice was an easy one—Denny Overman, his next-door neighbor and best friend. Denny, like Beano, was no athlete, and had no experience with sports beyond collecting scores in his weekend job at the Barton *Chronicle*. But Beano knew he would have Denny's support and cooperation.

They were eating their lunches together in the cafeteria when Beano leaned across and, speaking softly, told Denny he was going to be coaching the Tigers.

"No kidding—you!" Denny exclaimed.

Beano grinned at Denny's shock and said, "Yes, no kidding—me!" Then he added, "Keep it to yourself, will you?"

"Sure."

"Look, I can't be the coach and the student manager at the same time. Will you take over the manager duties?"

Denny frowned. "I don't know anything about—"

"I can tell you what to do. Will you do it?"

Denny gave a little shrug. "Okay, sure."

"Good. Show up in the dressing room after the last class."

Denny nodded. Then he shook his head. "I can't believe this," he said.

"I can't either," Beano said.

In the early afternoon, the rumor began circulating that Coach Pritchard had died in the hospital of his injuries. Suddenly it was everywhere around the school. It quickly took on such credence that Principal Tyler went on the intercom and announced to the entire school that he had a current report on Coach Pritchard's condition. He was still critical, but stable.

As Principal Tyler was reading his statement over the intercom, Beano was seated at a desk in his English class. He was scribbling furiously in a notebook. Miss Murphy, if she'd noticed, undoubtedly would have concluded that Beano was recording her every comment on Shakespeare's *Macbeth*. It never would have entered her mind that Beano was reworking the practice plan he had outlined in study hall.

Then, just before the final bell of the day, Principal Tyler's voice came on the intercom again.

"There will be a special meeting of the football team in the dressing room after school," he said.

When the bell rang, Beano gathered up his books, got to his feet, and said aloud to no one in particular, "Well, here we go."

The girl behind him, Nancy Whitman, said, "Huh?"

Beano looked at her. "Nothing," he said.

The dressing room was packed with players, all of them still in their street clothes and none of them making the first move to change into their practice uniforms.

Watching them from his perch on the training table, Beano concluded that after all of the rumors they had decided that Principal Tyler had called the meeting to announce the cancellation of the Carterville game. What else was there to do? The Tigers' coach was in the hospital critically injured, and there was no one to take his place. How does a team practice, and then play a game, without a coach? The players' conclusion was logical.

Even Beano had to admit it.

He spotted Denny Overman in the milling crowd. Nobody seemed to be questioning Denny's presence or tying it in any way to the coming announcement. Probably the players assumed Denny, a weekend employee of the Barton *Chronicle*, was there to report the announcement for the newspaper.

Then Principal Tyler walked in, followed by Mr. Custer.

The chatter among the players faded away, and thirty serious faces turned toward the two men.

Principal Tyler looked around the room, making sure he had everyone's attention. Then he got right to the point. "We are going to go ahead with the Carterville game," he said.

Some of the players exchanged glances, but the dressing room was so quiet that Beano thought he could hear people breathing from across the room.

"I have appointed Beano Hatton acting coach for this last game of the season," Principal Tyler said.

Suddenly nobody was even breathing.

Beano sat still as a statue on the training table, his thin arms folded over his chest, his head bowed a little, eyes fixed on a spot on the floor in front of him.

If the room had been silent before, what was

this? The silence was more silent than ever. A quantum leap in total silence, Beano thought.

Beano looked up at Principal Tyler and fought back an urge to shout: "Somebody—say something!"

Nobody did.

Finally, Principal Tyler said something. "Beano knows the team, he knows football, and he knows Coach Pritchard's system." He looked at the faces turned up toward him. "I know that Beano will have the cooperation of all of you. I know you want to defeat Carterville and make Coach Pritchard very proud of you."

Still, stunned silence.

Principal Tyler looked at Beano, smiled, and said, "Beano, it's yours."

Beano slid off the training table and drew himself up to his full five feet five inches of height and—weird!—wondered if Harry Truman had ever coached a football team.

He got that thought out of his mind and said, "We're already running late with practice because of this meeting. So get a hustle on, and I'll see you on the field."

With that, Beano walked out the door.

Chapter 3

Alone in the corridor outside the dressing room, Beano's first act as coach was to head for the water fountain. His mouth was dry and his stomach felt like a tangle of knots. He took a deep breath and was taking a large swallow of water when Principal Tyler and Mr. Custer emerged from the dressing room and turned toward him.

Principal Tyler looked incredulous. Had Beano Hatton really told the football players to "get a hustle on" and then walked out without a sign of a doubt that his order would be obeyed?

Mr. Custer was grinning.

Principal Tyler stepped forward, his right hand extended, and said, "Good luck."

Beano took the principal's hand and shook. He had never shaken hands with Principal Tyler before, or even with one of his teachers.

"I think I'll hang around," Mr. Custer said.

Beano looked at the two of them. Probably the principal and the teacher thought it a good idea to have a faculty member present, at least at the first practice conducted by the new acting coach. Beano said, "Sure."

Principal Tyler nodded and left.

"That was well done," Mr. Custer said, tilting his head toward the dressing room door and still grinning. He had clearly enjoyed the first minute of Beano's administration.

"I thought it might be better to leave them among themselves to overcome the initial shock," Beano said with a weak smile.

"Yes, good idea," Mr. Custer said. "You're off to a good start, Beano."

Beano took another deep breath, then extended his empty hands. "Yeah, great," he said. "I walked out and left my clipboard with the practice plan on it. Now I've got to go back in and get it."

Beano walked back to the dressing room, stopped for a fraction of a second, took a breath, and then shoved his way through the door.

He heard the buzz of conversation as he took his first step into the dressing room. Then—nothing. Suddenly, total silence again.

"C'mon, c'mon," he barked. "Get with it. We've got work—a lot of work—to do."

He walked down the aisle between gawking players and picked up his clipboard off the training table. Then he turned to walk back out.

Very few of the players had even begun to peel off their street clothes to change into their practice uniforms. They had stood in stunned silence, apparently, until Principal Tyler and Mr. Custer had followed the new acting coach out of the dressing room. Then they had burst forth with a gush of exclamations, questions, comments, and—maybe—complaints.

Beano stopped and turned to a player at random.

He gulped at the misfortune of his choice. The Tigers' starting left tackle, Bud Holland, was standing there. He was the largest player on the team. He stood six feet five inches tall, exactly one foot taller than Beano.

Beano was staring eye level at Bud's chest. But he went ahead. Beano looked up into Bud's face. Bud looked down into Beano's face.

"Have you forgotten how to change your clothes, Bud?" he said, and turned on his heel and walked out of the dressing room again.

He heard Bud's voice behind him. "Gee, Beano."

Yeah, Beano thought. Gee.

From the opening calisthenics through the last wind sprint at a few minutes before five thirty, Beano ran the Tigers through precisely the same light Monday drill he had seen Coach Pritchard preside over for three years.

That way, he figured, nobody could complain that anything had changed for the worse. And nobody did complain.

But there were changes, to be sure.

The most notable to Beano was the expressions on the faces of the players he knew so well. On this day their expressions were not the ones they wore under the guidance of Coach Pritchard.

Marty Tucker, the quarterback, for example, always tried to catch the coach's eye after a good or even an only-adequate play with an expression that openly requested a word or a nod of approval.

But today Marty Tucker did not seek Coach Beano Hatton's approval. Marty looked more as if he was trying to figure out whether someone—Beano Hatton, to be exact—had jumped over him, the quarterback, in seniority and authority. Was

Beano Hatton—of all people—going to tell him, Marty Tucker, which plays to call? Marty's answer was written on his face.

Under the stern practice-field gaze of Coach Pritchard, a lot of the players wore undisguised expressions of anxiety, if not fear. The starters were worried about losing their slots to eager second-stringers. And all worried about the embarrassment of a tongue lashing from the coach in front of their teammates.

Beano had watched it all for three years from the sidelines, and he saw the difference on this day.

Some of the players, following the lead of Edwin Deere, the chubby junior who played guard, acted as if the whole scene was a big joke. They called Beano "Coach Hatton." And one piped up with: "Coach Hatton, will you start me on Friday night?" Beano returned such remarks with his best version of a cold stare.

There were a lot of confused looks from players trying to decide whether to accept or reject the acting coach. One of these was Bud Holland, the big left tackle who looked as if he could not believe what he was seeing. Another was Larry Slider, the linebacker and cocaptain.

Another change was the crowd of fans attending the practice.

When the first players finally came out of the dressing room, Beano and Mr. Custer were standing at the end-zone sideline, and a large crowd of students was strung out alongside them. They had come from their last class to see what, if anything, was happening to their now-leaderless football team. The students knew nothing of Principal Tyler's announcement to the team, so they waited and watched.

The appearance of Beano at the end-zone sideline was nothing unusual. He was, after all, the team's student manager. The presence of Mr. Custer might mean the teacher was taking over. Or it might not.

As the players jogged onto the field and lined up in the end zone for their warm-up calisthenics under the direction of Marty Tucker and Larry Slider, Beano and Mr. Custer were joined by Zip Logan, manager of the Barton radio station.

"Who's going to run the team?" he asked Mr. Custer.

"Beano."

Zip leaned around Mr. Custer and looked at the student manager. "Beano?" he said.

"Beano," repeated Mr. Custer.

Zip gave Beano another glance and then left, heading for his car. Beano saw him in the car talking on a cellular telephone. The word was going out to the radio listeners of Barton.

Then the crowd got bigger as the townspeople began to arrive. All through practice the townspeople and the students stood along the sidelines gawking. Moving around the field, Beano heard his name being spoken. Sometimes it was in a sort of astonished conversational tone: "It really *is* Beano!" Other times there were shouts of enthusiastic encouragement: "Hey, give it to 'em, Beano!"

By the time the team was doing the closing wind sprints, with the sun going down and the temperature falling with the advance of darkness, the crowd had dwindled away to nobody.

At some point Mr. Custer had departed, but Beano did not know when.

Beano waved the last of the players off the practice field and toward the dressing room, and stalked inside behind them.

It was time for his speech. But that, he decided, would have to wait for a large swallow of water from the fountain in the corridor. He drank the water, straightened his shoulders, took a deep breath, and walked into the dressing room.

"Let me have your attention for just a moment before you head into the showers," he said.

A couple of groans went up, followed by a giggle or two.

Beano ignored them and waited until the room was quiet.

"We had a good practice out there today, and it proves that we can do it," he said. "If I didn't think we could do it, I wouldn't be standing here now. And I assume that all of you think we can do it too, or you wouldn't be here either." He paused. "Working together, we can win this game for Coach Pritchard." He gave a little nod and said, "Thank you."

The dressing room was strangely quiet as Beano, not looking at the face of any player, walked down the aisle to the training table and perched himself on it to wait until the last player had showered, dressed, and left.

When Beano and Denny turned out the lights in the dressing room and stepped into the corridor, planning to walk the eight blocks to their homes together, Beano saw John Bagley waiting for him.

Beano took a breath and said to Denny, "You go ahead, I'll see you tomorrow."

"Sure," Denny said, and walked on.

Beano turned to Mr. Bagley.

Mr. Bagley was editor, sports editor, photographer, and, probably, chief pressman—virtually the entire staff—of the Barton *Chronicle*. He was a small man, about Beano's height, with dark hair turning gray and a perpetual look of weariness about him. Beano knew who he was, of course, because everyone knew everyone else in Barton. But Beano had never exchanged even a word of greeting with Mr. Bagley.

The man gave him a friendly smile and said, "Big news, Beano. Can you give me a few minutes for some questions?"

"I . . . " Beano said, and stopped. He was not sure he wanted to be quoted in the *Chronicle*. The players were sure to read the story. What if he came off trying to sound like a big shot? He was going to have problems enough with the likes of Marty Tucker. He did not need more trouble.

"It'll just take a few minutes, Beano," Mr. Bagley said. Then he added, "I've already spoken to Principal Tyler, if that's what's concerning you." He smiled again. "Principal Tyler said he had no objections to an interview."

To Beano's surprise, the word "interview" chilled him. Nobody had ever interviewed him. He did not know what to say in an interview. And he did not know what to say to Mr. Bagley's request at this moment. So he said, "Sure, okay."

Mr. Bagley nodded encouragingly.

"In here," Beano said. He led Mr. Bagley back into the dressing room and flipped on the light switch. They sat facing each other on benches in front of the lockers.

Beano remembered one noticeable consistency in the *Chronicle* stories quoting Coach Pritchard: They never said much. Coach Pritchard always predicted a tough game. He always promised that the Tigers would give their best. He always said they were ready to play, and he hoped for victory. And he did not say much else. Well, Beano figured, he could say those things too.

Beano placed his school books and his clipboard with the practice schedule on the bench next to him, and Mr. Bagley drew a notebook from his overcoat pocket and a ballpoint pen from his shirt pocket.

"Were you surprised?"

That one was easy enough. "Yes," Beano said.

One after another, the questions seemed to Beano to be easy enough. Did you consider turning down Principal Tyler? "No." Are you nervous? "Yes." Will you do anything differently than Coach Pritchard? "I hope not."

And then: "Will you call most of the plays from

the sidelines, as Coach Pritchard always did, or will you let Marty Tucker call his own plays?"

Beano hesitated. He could see Marty Tucker looking through the story for that question—and answer. Finally Beano said, "Probably I'll call some of the plays, based on the game plan I'll have drawn up. But Marty will understand the game plan, and Marty does understand Coach Pritchard's system, so he will know which plays to call a lot of the time."

Beano watched Mr. Bagley write down his words.

Then, inevitably: "What do the players think about all of this: Beano Hatton, the student manager, taking over as acting coach?"

Beano smiled. He had no trouble with the question. He said, "I don't know what they think. I haven't had a chance to talk with any of them about it."

Mr. Bagley pulled a small camera out of his coat pocket and took a picture of Beano seated on the training table, a smile on his face.

Chapter 4

The walk home through the darkness—eight blocks of tree-lined streets—afforded Beano his first opportunity of the day to do what he did best: think.

He had gotten his nickname in fifth grade when an enthusiastic teacher kept applauding Beano's incisive answers by exclaiming: "That's using the ol' bean."

The other kids thought it hilariously funny and began calling him Beano.

As for Beano, he latched on to the nickname because he considered it, though a little strange, to be a vast, vast improvement over his given name of Hubert.

It was around the same time that Hubert Hatton discovered to his dismay that, while he was good at "using the ol' bean," he was never going to be an athlete. Not only was he shorter and skinnier than everyone else, his body refused to take orders from his brain. He was, as they said, uncoordinated. While others told their hands to catch the ball and the hands did catch the ball, Hubert Hatton's hands let the ball hit him in the face.

So, about the time he became Beano Hatton, he decided to give up the athletic life in favor of a life of thinking—and quickly discovered, to his delight, that thinking was needed in sports every bit as much as running, catching, and throwing. Thinking won games—football, baseball, basketball.

The position for Beano—who could not run, catch, or throw but who loved the thinking involved in sports—was the job of student manager. He signed up in the tenth grade.

Now a senior, he was sure he had enjoyed his three years of watching Coach Pritchard work out tactics and strategy, trying to match him thought for thought, every bit as much as the runners and passers. Beano enjoyed thinking.

And now, walking along, he was thinking.

He decided rather quickly that, yes, he was going to devise the game plan and call most of the plays from the sidelines against Carterville. He, and not Marty Tucker. Coach Pritchard drew up a game plan and called most of the plays. He did not leave those important items to Marty Tucker's judgment. And why was that? Because Coach Pritchard did not trust Marty Tucker's judgment, that was why.

So what made Beano Hatton, who was not Coach Pritchard, any better than Marty Tucker, the quarterback? Beano unconsciously nodded his head at the question. Principal Tyler had named Beano, not Marty, acting coach. Yes, Marty was strong, a quick and fast runner, an adequate passer, and Beano was none of those things. But Beano could think better, and Principal Tyler knew it.

Then it was settled: Beano, and not Marty, would draw up the game plan and decide on the plays to be run.

Any thought of Marty Tucker immediately widened into the broader question of how to gain the confidence of the players—and quickly.

For Beano, the most troubling aspect of the whole afternoon had been the reaction of the players—the stunned silence at Principal Tyler's announcement, the buzz of conversation that Beano walked into when he returned to the dressing room, the looks that he was drawing from the players on the practice field, the flat silence his short speech after practice had inspired.

Beano Hatton knew he was not one of them. The players were the players, and the student manager was, well, a guy who couldn't be a player. The players hung out together like they were members of a club from which others, including Beano, were excluded. Beano hardly knew Marty Tucker, Larry Slider—any of them—outside the dressing room, the playing field, and the occasional class they had together. No, Beano wasn't one of the guys on the team.

As Beano walked under a streetlight, watching his shadow leap out in front of him on the sidewalk, he let the question of gaining the players' confidence without being one of the guys roll around in his mind.

The answer was simple, Beano concluded.

He did not need to be one of them in order to coach the Tigers against the Carterville Bobcats. Coach Pritchard was not one of the guys; he was the coach. Beano also was not one of the guys, and he had to somehow get himself accepted as the coach. To do this, he needed some test he could pass to demonstrate that he was in charge and that he was capable. Principal Tyler's announcement was the formal word. Now it was up to Beano to make it a fact.

Beano turned the last corner and saw, a block away, his house, the porch light on, awaiting his arrival.

He knew that his mother was there, probably setting the table for dinner, and his younger brother was there, probably demanding dinner right now—and his father, as usual, was not there, but instead was in Cleveland or St. Louis or somewhere on business.

From the moment Beano stepped into the house and closed the front door behind him, the evening was like no other in his life.

For one thing, his younger brother, Jeremy, greeted him with an enthusiastic shout. "Hey! Are you really the Tigers' football coach?"

This was not like Jeremy at all. At age seven, Jeremy had long ago decided that his older brother, if not actually in conspiracy with adults, tended to side with them. Beano, he often said, even acted like an adult. As a result, Jeremy offered Beano the same bland stares, the same noncommittal grunts, that he gave to adults. But this time Jeremy was different.

Beano looked at his brother's grinning, excited face. "That's what they tell me," he said.

Mrs. Hatton came walking in from the kitchen as Beano was pulling off his jacket. "Are you all right?" she asked.

Beano grinned and nodded. His mother always viewed any unexpected development as fraught with danger, probably damaging to the health. Beano hung up his jacket on a peg on the inside of the closet door.

"I heard about it on the radio," his mother said. "Why didn't you call?"

Beano looked at the ceiling. Sure, he was going to end the meeting in Principal Tyler's office by asking to use the telephone to call his mother. Good grief!

Beano brought his line of sight down from the ceiling, looked at his mother, and said, "I didn't have a chance to call. It turned out to be a pretty busy day, you know."

"Practice had already started when I heard about it. Zip Logan said he was broadcasting from the practice field."

"Actually from his car," Beano said.

"Well, anyway, I was tempted to drive around to the school to see for myself."

This time Beano said it aloud: "Good grief!"

"What?"

"I mean that I'm glad you didn't," Beano said.

The last thing Acting Coach Beano Hatton needed was his mother overseeing the first practice from the sidelines.

His mother smiled. "I know. That's why I didn't do it." She turned and headed back toward the kitchen. "Come on, dinner is just about ready."

"Wow!" Jeremy said, still gawking up at Beano. He apparently had stifled his excitement as long as possible.

Beano gave Jeremy a glance as he headed for the kitchen, marveling at his brother's transformation.

Through dinner at the round kitchen table, Beano related the day's happenings—the meeting in Principal Tyler's office, some of the conversation with Mr. Custer in the cafeteria, Principal Tyler's announcement to the team, and carefully selected bits about practice. But he left out any mention of his concern about the players' views.

So his mother asked, "How are the players accepting you?"

Beano took a breath. "They were surprised, same as I was. It's too early to tell what they really think." He managed a little grin that he hoped shielded his feelings. "I think it will come out before the week is over."

Then, changing the subject, he quickly asked,

"Do you think Dad will be calling tonight?"

In his travels as a manufacturer's representative, Beano's father usually called home a couple of times a week.

Beano's mother took a moment to think, then said, "I doubt if he'll be calling tonight. The convention in Chicago ended last night, and he was driving to St. Louis. Probably he'll arrive late and won't call." She paused, then added, "If he doesn't call tonight, we'll call him in St. Louis tomorrow night."

Beano wished that his father was home this night. He needed to talk to someone who knew he was more than a water boy, as the players thought, and less than a genius, as Principal Tyler and Mr. Custer seemed to think.

"Will he be home by Friday night, for the game?"

"I'm sure."

Beano took his last bite, and just in time. The telephone rang.

"Maybe that's your father now," Mrs. Hatton said as she got up and walked across to the telephone on the far wall of the kitchen.

But Beano knew the caller was not his father from the first words his mother spoke: "Yes, Mr. Tyler." She glanced across at Beano as she spoke.

"Yes, we've finished dinner. . . . Yes, very surprising news, and exciting. . . . Yes, he's right here."

Beano got up and walked across and took the telephone from his mother.

"I heard that practice went well, Beano," Principal Tyler said.

"Yes, I think it was all right."

"I was going to drop by myself, but I got caught up in a meeting that dragged on until after five thirty. Maybe I'll be able to make it tomorrow."

"Yes. Fine."

"Good, good."

Beano waited.

"I just wanted to check with you, Beano, and tell you that if you need any time out of class—for preparation, you know—well, it'll be approved. If I'm not available, Mr. Custer will explain to your teachers."

"All right," Beano said. "I probably will need some time. I'll have to lay out the practice schedule each day, and I'm going to have to begin drawing up a game plan."

"Anything you need."

"Thank you."

"And, well, again, good luck."

"Thank you."

Beano replaced the receiver and stood for a

moment, his hand still on the telephone. Beano mused at the oddness of his situation. Just how often does the principal of a high school call a student and wish him luck? More to the point, did the principal have any idea how badly the student needed some good luck?

Then the telephone rang under his hand. Beano lifted the receiver. "Hello."

"Beano? Todd."

Todd Bowman was the Tigers' first-string running back. He was also Marty Tucker's best friend and his major competitor for star of the team. Beano had never spoken with Todd on the telephone before—nor with Marty, either, for that matter—and he idly thought how different Todd sounded.

"Yes, Todd?"

"Beano, some of us were talking after practice, and well, you know, with Marty having complete control over the offense, this being his second year as a starter and all, and . . . "

Beano listened silently to Todd's rambling, disjointed sentence. Miss Murphy, Beano's English teacher, would have been appalled. She would have knocked out half the words. She would have replaced half the commas with periods. And then she would have proclaimed a great improvement in clarity. But Beano was having no trouble with the clarity of Todd's point. He knew exactly where Todd was going with his tangled monologue.

Beano finally interrupted him. "Todd," he said.

"Yes, what?"

"Todd, the answer is no."

"But you haven't even heard me out, and all of us—"

"Wait, Todd."

The telephone line went silent.

Beano said, "Todd, you're saying that you and Marty and some of the others have decided that Marty should run the offense without interference from me. But Todd, *I* am the coach. *I* am going to draw up the game plan. And *I* am going to call the plays I think I ought to call. So my answer is—no."

Again silence on the telephone line.

Beano realized that he was holding the telephone in a fierce grip and that his teeth were clamped together so tightly that a jaw muscle was twitching.

Finally Todd spoke. His voice took on a menacing quality. "Beano, you're going to need the cooperation of the players if you hope to pull this off, and Marty thinks—"

"I expect to have the cooperation of the players," Beano said. "And as for what Marty thinks, I'll discuss that with Marty, if he likes."

After a moment Todd said, "Okay."

"See you tomorrow," Beano said, and hung up the telephone.

"Trouble?" Mrs. Hatton asked.

"Maybe."

Beano took a deep breath. No, maybe not trouble. If this kind of confrontation was inevitable—and Beano figured that it was—better for it to come now, on Monday, rather than on Friday night.

Beano looked at his mother. "If there are any other telephone calls for me, please tell them that the acting coach of the Barton High Tigers is doing his calculus homework."

Chapter 5

When Beano arrived at Barton High the next morning, he did indeed have the calculus assignment completed, but it had been slow going. Seated at his desk in his room, his notebook and calculus textbook both open, he repeatedly found the numbers blurring and his attention focused on the darkness outside the window. There were so many thoughts—none of them involving calculus—swirling through his mind.

The one bit of good news was that the telephone did not ring again. Todd Bowman did not call back to resume his argument. Marty Tucker did not call to take up his case for himself. Nobody called at all.

But what did that mean? Was it really good news? Maybe it was bad.

Lying in bed later that night, Beano turned over all the bad possibilities in his mind.

What if Marty Tucker quit—just quit—and refused to play? Marty always joined the basketball team at the end of football season. He could just walk out on the football team and join the basketball team a week early. It wouldn't be a big deal for him. Basketball was bigger than football at Barton High, and so plenty of people would probably applaud Marty's move.

But how does a football team play without its quarterback? Beano thought about Dave Harris, the sophomore who was second-string quarterback behind Marty. Dave had not seen more than ten minutes of action all season.

And what if Todd Bowman quit with Marty? He probably would do it. They were best friends. How does a team play with both the quarterback and the running back missing?

Others might go too.

In one horrible scene his imagination conjured up, Beano saw himself at the sidelines with no players at all while the Carterville team was taking the field.

What would Beano say when the referee walked up to him and asked: "Where are your players?"

And the Barton High fans in the bleachers, what about them? Would they boo Beano? Sure they would. His mother and Jeremy and also probably his father would be sitting in the bleachers, terribly embarrassed. People around them, their friends, would give them funny looks.

Then the referee would declare a forfeit. What was the official score of a forfeited game? It was 1–0. Carterville High defeats Barton High by a score of 1–0. And then Beano would go home, never again to emerge and face the glares of the people around town.

Beano squeezed his eyes shut and finally dropped off to sleep.

Beano spotted Marty and Todd and a couple of other players standing together in the corridor when he walked through the front door of the school building.

They spotted him, too, and watched as he approached.

Beano took a deep breath, squared his shoulders, said, "Good morning," and walked past them.

None of the players said anything, not even a greeting, but Beano could feel their eyes on his back as he went on down the corridor.

Beano's greeting—friendly enough but a little cool, a little aloof—was the first demonstration of the new Acting Coach Beano Hatton. He had awakened in the morning with a solution born of three years of watching Coach Pritchard handle the players. Coach Pritchard had a way of making each player feel that he was important—but not indispensable. Coach Pritchard always seemed to be saying, without actually putting it into words, "If you play for the Tigers, you are very important. If you choose not to play, so what, go ahead and quit; the Tigers still will be there for the game." Coach Pritchard's air was unmistakable. Beano's was going to be the same. Marty or Todd or anyone else was important only if he played. They were unimportant if they quit. Beano might have to insert Bud Holland at quarterback—heaven help them—but if so, then okay.

Beano turned into Mr. Custer's classroom. It was five minutes before the bell for the first class. Mr. Custer was alone in the classroom, shuffling some papers on his desk.

"Good morning, Coach Hatton," Mr. Custer said with a smile.

"Good morning," Beano said. He put his books and his football clipboard on a front-row desk and turned back to the teacher. "Principal Tyler said I could take some classroom time for preparation. He said you would arrange the absence with the teacher."

"Yes. What is it you want to do?"

"Well, actually, I don't need to miss any classes, but I would like to get excused from study hall— third period—and find a place where I can make a couple of telephone calls. I need to talk to some people who probably are only available in the morning."

"Third period? Is that Mrs. Matthews' study hall?"

"Yes."

"I think that can be arranged." He smiled. "I'll talk with her."

Beano nodded, and waited.

"And—?" Mr. Custer asked.

"This morning I'll need a place with a telephone."

"Yes, you mentioned a telephone. Why a telephone?"

"I don't know the first thing about the Carterville Bobcats. I want to call the coaches of a couple of teams that have played them."

Mr. Custer frowned, seeming unsure. "Did

Coach Pritchard do that sort of thing?"

"I don't know, but I can't think of any other way to find out about them."

Mr. Custer's frown faded and he finally chuckled. "All right," he said. "There's a telephone in the athletic office, you know. You can use Coach Pritchard's desk."

"Will the others . . . ?"

The three coaches—Coach Pritchard, Coach Beardsley, and Coach Wyandotte—shared the athletic office, each with a desk. Would Coach Beardsley and Coach Wyandotte welcome Beano Hatton even in his role as acting football coach?

"The office should be free," Mr. Custer said. "The coaches will be in the gym with phys-ed classes." He looked at Beano and added, "I'll tell them that you're going to be using the office."

Beano nodded. "Thanks," he said.

"Anything else?"

Beano shrugged and gave a little smile. "Not that I know of," he said.

"Any problems so far?"

Beano was sure that Mr. Custer was referring to problems with the players. But he figured that those kinds of problems—if, indeed, there were problems—belonged to him, and there was nothing Mr. Custer could do to help. So Beano shook his head and said, "Not that I know of."

The bell rang and Beano scooped his books and clipboard off the desk.

"Let me know if there's anything I can do," Mr. Custer said.

"Thanks."

Beano sat at Coach Pritchard's desk in the athletic office at the beginning of the third period. Suddenly he recognized an obstacle to checking out the strengths and weaknesses of the Carterville Bobcats. There was nothing in sight—not under the glass on the desktop nor on the bulletin board on the wall—to indicate which teams the Bobcats had played, much less which teams they had defeated and which they had lost to.

After looking around, Beano sat down again at the desk, feeling a bit of a fool. Then he called the *Chronicle* and asked for Mr. Bagley. Surely the *Chronicle* had the schedule of an area team such as Carterville, and probably the scores of the Bobcats' games.

"Mr. Bagley is in the press room," said a woman's voice.

"This is important," Beano said.

"Who's calling?"

Beano watched the clock on the opposite wall

ticking away the minutes of his free period. "Beano Hatton," he said.

"Just a minute."

Mr. Bagley came on the line. "Beano, yes, what is it? This is my busiest time of the day."

Beano explained what he needed and then listened to silence on the line. Finally Mr. Bagley said, "All right. Hold on."

Beano nervously tapped a pencil on his notebook while he waited.

Then Mr. Bagley came back on the line. "The Bobcats have lost three games, same as the Tigers."

"That's what I want—the teams that beat them."

Beano jotted down the names of the three schools and asked, "Do you have the coaches' names?"

"They're in the high school athletic association's handbook." Then, when Beano did not speak, Mr. Bagley added, "Just a minute, I'll look 'em up."

Beano wrote the appropriate coach's name next to each of the three schools. He wanted to ask if the handbook offered telephone numbers but decided he had pressed Mr. Bagley far enough. He thanked him, hung up, and looked at his list.

* * *

"Hello?" The tone of the voice on the telephone made a question of the greeting. Then, "Who is this?"

"Coach Morse, this is, uh, Hubert"—the hated name seemed to carry more weight than the nickname—"Hatton, at Barton High."

"Yes."

"You know, I suppose, that Coach Pritchard was seriously injured in a traffic accident last weekend and is hospitalized."

"Yes. How is Henry?"

"He's still in intensive care, but it looks as if he's going to be all right."

"That's good. I'm glad to hear it." Then: "What can I do for you?"

Beano sucked in a deep breath. "Well, I'm standing in for Coach Pritchard in our last game, against Carterville, this Friday night, and you beat Carterville, but I don't know anything about the Bobcats, and I thought maybe you might be willing to help me with some information."

"What did you say your name was?"

"Hubert Hatton."

"We've never met."

"No."

"Are you faculty . . . or what?"

Beano unconsciously shook his head. He

wished that a shake of his head would suffice for an answer. But he knew it wouldn't, not on the telephone. So he said, "I'm the student manager."

"Really?"

"Really."

There was a moment of silence on the line. Then Beano heard a burst of laughter. He frowned.

Coach Morse said, "Son, you just tell me what you want to know, and I'll try to give you the answers."

Chapter 6

Beano replaced the telephone in its cradle, ending his conversation with the second of the coaches whose teams had defeated the Carterville Bobcats.

Both coaches—first Coach Morse of Barrow Meadows High and then Coach Patton of Warrington High—had listened to his plea and then opened their minds to him, pouring out even more information than Beano had hoped for.

His left hand remained on the telephone while he scanned the scrawled notes on the legal-size pad of yellow paper. He had notes on everything from style of play and tendencies in critical situations to individual talents and weaknesses. With a little study, he was going to know the Carterville Bobcats as well as he knew his own Barton High Tigers.

The thought crossed his mind that, yes, this must be what Coach Pritchard did—call the coaches of the teams that had played the Tigers' opponents. It explained how he so mysteriously came to know secrets about the opposing team.

Beano was looking at the name of the third coach on the list when suddenly the bell rang ending the period. Beano gave a little jump at the startling interruption to his thoughts and jerked his hand off the telephone as if it was red-hot.

He looked up at the large clock on the wall, confirming the time signaled by the jangling bell.

There was no time left to call the third coach. But it didn't really matter. The two he had talked to—Coach Morse and Coach Patton—had made essentially the same points. Probably the third coach, too, would say the same things.

Beano gathered his books and his clipboard, stood up, replaced Coach Pritchard's chair under the desk, and left the desk as he had found it.

When he stepped out the door of the office, he spotted Coach Beardsley and Coach Wyandotte approaching the office together from the end of the corridor. The Barton High grapevine reported from time to time that the two coaches, both just a couple of years out of college, were dating. Beano reflected that he wasn't going to have any time this week for evaluating rumors on the Barton High grapevine.

"Good morning," Beano said as he approached.

They both gave him a curious look. They had seen him emerging from the coaches' office. Possibly the word had not reached them that he had permission to use Coach Pritchard's desk. Then, at the last minute, they smiled and said together, "Good morning, Beano."

Beano turned at the end of the corridor and headed up the steps leading to the first floor and Mr. Custer's American History class, his last class before the lunch period.

Students going down the steps, heading to their phys-ed class in the gym, called out to Beano, some referring to him with a laugh as "Coach."

Beano, hardly seeing or hearing them, responded almost automatically with "Hi!" or "Hey!" and continued on his way.

He was lost in his thoughts. The two coaches had provided really remarkable detail. There were little weaknesses of the Carterville team to be exploited. There were strengths to be avoided or blunted. Coach Morse had even gone a step further, suggesting to Beano how the weaknesses might be exploited and how the strengths might be avoided. Coach Morse had, in effect, given Beano a crash course in coaching strategy.

All of this was turning over in Beano's mind as he reached the top of the stairs. Then, suddenly, a single thought clicked into his brain and stopped him in his tracks for a moment.

True, Beano had received useful information on the Carterville Bobcats from the two coaches. He had gotten tips on how to gain yardage against their defense, advice on how to stop their attack, and Coach Morse's strategy lesson.

But without realizing it, he had gotten something more, something vitally important.

Acting Coach Beano Hatton now knew more things—the really important things—about the Carterville Bobcats than any of the Barton High players did. Armed with that knowledge, Beano could run the practice sessions with authority, set the game plan without question, and direct the team on the basis of what he alone knew.

Beano was almost smiling at the new strength that came with his discovery when he saw Walton Custer standing outside his classroom door. Mr. Custer always stood outside before class, nodding or speaking a welcome to the students entering.

Beano veered across the corridor toward the classroom door.

"Did you speak with the coaches?" Mr. Custer
asked.

"Two of them, yes."

"Were they helpful?"

"Very," Beano said.

At noon, Beano dropped off his books with the
clipboard at the table where he and Denny always
ate and moved into the food line. When Beano
arrived back at the table with his tray, Denny,
ahead of him, was already there with a couple of
other students.

They were discussing the theatrics of Miss
Murphy's Shakespeare recitations in English class.

Beano ate his lunch, watching and listening but
hardly hearing the chatter and the occasional
chuckle at the teacher's overdramatic presenta-
tions. His mind, far from being on either Miss
Murphy or Shakespeare, was on the penciled notes
on the yellow pages clamped to the clipboard at his
left.

Denny, as if sensing Beano's preoccupation,
asked, "Is there anything you need me to do?"

Beano brought his mind back to the group at
the table and smiled at his friend. "If you can keep

Miss Murphy from looking at me in class this afternoon, that'll help. I need to get some notes together before practice."

One of the other students said, "When she gets that faraway look in her eyes, I don't think she even knows we're there."

When Beano had taken the last bite of his food and drained the last drop from his milk carton, he got to his feet, scooped up his books and the clipboard, and said, "Got to go. Got to get started on the notes."

"So long, coach," one of the students called out.

First to arrive in the dressing room, Beano took his perch on the training table. From there, without comment, he watched the arriving players. Some of them streaming into the dressing room called out greetings to Beano. Unsmiling, he acknowledged them with a slight bobbing of his head.

All of them to some degree still wore stunned expressions of disbelief on their faces. Beano Hatton—little Beano, who brought out the water—coaching the Barton High Tigers football team? Impossible!

More important to Beano was the fact that all of them were there. Marty Tucker entered with a blank-faced nod in Beano's direction and went to his locker. At least he hadn't received the bad news from Todd Bowman the night before and decided to go across the hall and explain to Coach Beardsley why he was ready to join the basketball team now. Todd entered behind Marty, frowned at Beano, and went straight to his locker and began undressing.

Edwin Deere, the junior guard with the everpresent smirk, sang out, "Hey, coach," as he came through the door. Beano responded with a small grin. It was impossible not to smile at Edwin.

Beano double-checked with a glance around the room. All of the players were there.

Just as the first of the players was ready for practice, the dressing-room door opened and Principal Tyler walked in.

Smiling, he gave the room a sweeping glance—much the same as Beano had and probably for the same reason, Beano thought—and then he spoke.

"Coach Pritchard has been removed from the intensive-care unit at the hospital, which is indeed good news," he said. "I've just come from a brief visit with him, and he sends his best wishes, and says he knows you will beat Carterville."

After a brief pause he said, "Have a good practice." Then, with a smiling nod in Beano's direction, he left as suddenly as he had appeared.

Except for a few murmured comments, the room was quiet again. Beano felt he ought to say something, so he gave a little wave of the arm and announced, "That was welcome news to us all . . . and now we've got to set about doing what Coach Pritchard asked: Beat Carterville."

Somebody said, "Right," but otherwise quiet settled over the room again as everyone finished changing.

When the first player dressed for practice started out of the dressing room—it was Art Fleming, an end—Beano called out, "Hold up a minute, please, before leaving." Art stopped at the door and turned and waited. Others glanced at Beano with questioning expressions.

A voice sounded in the silence, "Our new coach likes to make speeches." Beano looked in the direction of the voice as a few players chuckled. The speaker was Edwin Deere, naturally.

"I've got a couple of things to explain," Beano said, "and I want to do it in here, privately, instead of out there in front of whoever's dropped by to watch practice."

Nobody spoke, not even Edwin Deere.

"First, the offense," Beano said, looking straight at Marty. Marty's face wore a look of indifference. Or maybe it was strained tolerance, an unspoken statement that nothing Beano might say was worth the time spent listening.

Beano kept his eyes on Marty. "Carterville's linebackers like to blitz, which will give us an opportunity to complete short passes over center and make good gains with draw plays and traps. Marty, I want you to work the offense on those kinds of plays out there this afternoon."

Marty frowned in puzzlement. How did Beano Hatton know these things?

"Okay, offense can go out. Marty, start them on their calisthenics, will you? Defense, please stay a moment."

The room was deadly silent. Nobody moved. Marty stared at Beano, his mouth half open. Beano stared back.

Then, with a nod, Marty got to his feet and headed for the door, with others following.

When the last of the offense had passed through the door, Beano scanned the remaining players, the Barton High Tigers defensive unit.

"You're in for a grueling night," Beano said. "The Bobcats play a very straightforward, conservative style of football. Lots of line plunges and end runs—and no tricks. Also very few, if any, passes. They're not fast or explosive, but they're strong, and they keep pounding away. So prepare yourselves to hit somebody—and then somebody else—time and again."

Several members of the defensive unit were now giving the Marty Tucker stare—wide-eyed, with mouth half-open. How did Beano Hatton know these things? Others seemed to be coming to the realization that Beano Hatton had done for football what he always did for the classroom: his homework.

"We may switch our defense to add a third linebacker," Beano said. "We'll work on that some—a third linebacker." He looked at a player leaning against a locker. "It'll be you, Clark." To Beano's surprise, Clark Gray, a substitute linebacker, nodded as if the announcement had come from Coach Pritchard. "But we'll start the game with our usual two linebackers and see how it goes."

Beano slid off the training table and said, "Okay, let's go to work."

The players shuffled toward the door and filed through, Beano waiting and then following the last one out.

Chapter 7

Beano, coming out of the school building with his clipboard in his hand for the short walk across to the practice field, was not prepared for what he saw.

He had expected to see Marty and the members of the offensive unit beginning their loosening-up drills at one end of the field. And Marty did have them lined up, bending and stretching.

He had expected to see the members of the defensive unit, arriving a few minutes later, taking their places in the line and beginning to exercise. And they were, indeed, approaching and taking up positions.

The unusually large crowd of people around the practice field, while not really expected, did not surprise Beano. He knew that he was a curiosity—

a student manager with a coach's clipboard in his hand instead of a water bottle.

What *did* startle Beano was the knot of people standing just off the corner of the end zone—some of them with television cameras. One of the men was Mr. Bagley, who was now pointing out Beano to the others.

Beano knew instantly what he was facing. The same attraction that had drawn a lot of students and townspeople to the practice field had also drawn a couple of video crews from television stations.

Beano glanced at the players lined up in the end zone. They too had spotted the television crews and recognized them for what they were. Television crews were hardly a common occurrence at the practice sessions of the Barton High Tigers. This was something really new, and exciting.

The players were bending, stretching, straightening up—and gawking at the people with the cameras. Edwin Deere had simply quit the exercise drill and was standing, facing the television crews, just staring. Others were beginning to do the same.

Almost instinctively Beano looked around at the people standing at the edge of the practice field.

He searched for Principal Tyler's face, or Mr.
Custer's, or any teacher's. They were the ones to
deal with television crews. Not the student manager, even one who was the acting head coach. But he
did not see Principal Tyler or Mr. Custer or any
school official.

Beano took a deep breath and headed toward
the television crews at the corner of the end zone.
On the way he waved his clipboard at the players
and shouted, "Keep going."

Turning back, he saw that one of the camera
crews was taping his approach to the group. Beano
avoided looking into the lens of the camera.

A lot of the spectators edged toward the group.
Probably they wanted to hear what transpired. Or
maybe they hoped to get their faces in the camera's
line of sight and see themselves on their screens at
home tonight.

When he was ten feet from them, Beano said, "I
can't allow you to film any of our practice session."

The flat statement—a definite order—from the
skinny little fellow with the glasses seemed to surprise the television crews. Nobody said anything
for a moment, and by that time Beano was standing in front of them, up close.

The two crews were from Fort Wayne television stations. Beano recognized the station call letters plastered on their equipment.

"We won't bother anyone," one of them said. "We just want to shoot some frames of you in action."

"The networks are interested," another one said. "It's big news—a student coaching the team."

Beano wished that Principal Tyler or Mr. Custer would appear. But they didn't. He looked at Mr. Bagley and decided he would be of no help; he appeared impressed by the television crews and interested in what was happening—but nothing else.

Beano tried to think of what Coach Pritchard would do. Then he thought he knew.

"The answer is no," Beano said, "for two reasons.

"First, you'll distract the players. We've got a game on Friday night that would be tough under the best of circumstances, and we're not in the best of circumstances, as you know. The players need to concentrate on their practice. We don't need distractions.

"And second, presumably you want the tape to play on television, and I don't want the Carterville coach and all his players to be able to sit at home and watch our team practice on television."

Beano did not notice until he had finished that the other camera crew was taping his statement from off to the side.

"Well," said the man who seemed to be the spokesperson for the two crews, "how about just some footage of you, then. We won't shoot any of the actual drills."

"You've already got footage of me," Beano said, looking at the man and camera still focusing in on him.

The television people looked around at one another in silence, and Beano waited, wondering what to do if they simply refused.

Then a couple of them nodded questioningly, and the two men with cameras said, almost together, "Yeah, I've got him."

The self-appointed spokesperson turned to Beano and said with a smile, "Okay, coach, we'll honor your request."

Beano gave a little jerk of his head and turned and walked onto the practice field, trying to demonstrate to the television crews and the team members alike that the matter was settled.

"Let's go! Let's go!" Beano shouted at the players who had stopped completely and turned to watch the confrontation.

"Am I going to be on television?" Edwin Deere

called out as Beano approached.

Beano ignored Edwin. He spoke to Marty. "Finish 'em up here and we'll run some plays. I've got one for you that you've never run before, and it's going to take some work."

The quarterback gaped down at Beano. Beano looked up at him through his glasses. Then Marty's expression turned from surprise to protest. He started to say something.

But the acting coach had turned and walked away.

Beano set up the defense in the new three-line-backer configuration, placing Clark Gray on the right, Larry Slider in the middle, and Chickie Townsend on the left. He spread the outside line-backers, Clark and Chickie, wide one step. Then he nodded to Dave Harris, Marty's substitute at quarterback, and the second-string backfield began running plays into the line.

Beano stood and watched for a minute, telling Dave, "Throw one now and then, just to keep the defensive backs awake, okay?"

Beano sent Randy Wolfe, the placekicker, to the far end of the field to practice extra-point kicks and short field goals. Then he walked across and turned his attention to Marty and the offensive unit.

"Short, quick passes over center and some draw plays," Beano told Marty. "Like I said, the Carterville linebackers love to blitz. We'll go over 'em and past 'em."

Marty eyed Beano sharply, and Beano was sure for a moment that the quarterback was going to challenge him. Beano glared back, ready for a challenge. If Marty said, "How do you know?" Beano was tempted to say, "I know because the coach always knows." Beano knew that would be Coach Pritchard's answer. But Beano knew he was not Coach Pritchard and should not give the quarterback that kind of put-down answer.

But Marty, after glaring at him a moment, said nothing and turned to the task. Maybe, Beano thought, Marty also knew what Coach Pritchard's answer would be and didn't want to chance getting it from Beano.

Play resumed.

"Once more, once more," Beano called after each play.

Marty was good at throwing the short pass. He was big enough and strong enough for long passes, but had trouble with accuracy. On short passes, though, he threaded the needle most of the time. The right end, Art Fleming, and the wide receiver, Joe Burgess, hung on to most of them. The more Beano saw, the better he felt.

After almost every play, Marty turned to Beano with an expression that was half questioning and half protesting. Marty was, Beano knew, anticipating the "play you've never run before" and was ready to issue an instant objection. The quarterback was not about to buy some goofy play dreamed up by a pipsqueak student manager who had never run the ball, even in practice. We'll see, Beano told himself.

Near the end of practice, just before the time when Coach Pritchard would always put the Tigers through brief punting and kickoff drills, Beano called a halt and walked into the middle of the backfield.

Marty knew that this was it—the fact was stamped all over his face. So was his defiance.

Beano was armed with his recollection of Coach Morse's words on the telephone from Barrow Meadows High: "Carterville tries to block almost every punt instead of dropping back to help their receiver, and they've had some luck. I think a fake punt and run around end might go a long way, with those Carterville guys all charging forward. We didn't use it on them, but we didn't have to. It will probably work, though."

Beano gestured the players into a circle around him. They gathered in, some with puzzled looks, a couple with ill-concealed giggles: This was, after all, the student manager, Beano Hatton.

"To my knowledge, we've never run from punt formation," Beano said.

He saw Marty's face out of the corner of his eye. His expression seemed to say, "Aw, c'mon now." Other players were looking at Marty, seeking his lead. Marty was the Tigers' punter and would be bound to have something to say.

Beano plunged on. "Carterville almost always charges the punter, trying for a block. They sometimes even put ten players on the line of scrimmage. Very seldom do they drop back and protect the punt returner, hoping for a long gain." He paused. "Their punt returner is pretty slow-footed, for one thing."

Marty had held off as long as possible. "How do you know all this stuff about what's in the Carterville coach's mind? First that business about the linebackers blitzing all the time. And now this."

Beano gave Marty his very best version of an icy grin and let Coach Pritchard's familiar comeback move through his mind again: *I know because the coach always knows.* But Beano did not say it.

Instead Beano said, as matter-of-factly as he could, "I've done my homework on Carterville, Marty, as any coach would."

Marty looked surprised, and Beano thought for a moment he was going to ask where Beano was getting his information. But Marty simply looked around, as if expecting someone else to ask the question for him. Nobody did.

"So," Beano said, continuing as if Marty hadn't spoken, "we're going to be ready with a fake punt in case Carterville gives us reason to think it will work." He turned full face to Marty. "You are fast enough and strong enough to make it work."

Four times Beano lined up the offensive unit in punt formation. Marty ran to the left while linemen on that side imitated blocking. The right-side linemen posed as though letting their opponents charge through to no avail.

The first two times, Beano shouted at Marty, "Wider. Wider. Run wider." The runner had to go as far away as possible from the tacklers who were recovering and giving chase.

The third and fourth times, Marty did it the way Beano wanted.

"You're going to score a touchdown on that

play," a smiling Beano told the frowning Marty.

At the close of practice Beano sent the players running in to their showers and then stood on the field a moment and looked around. Most of the spectators had drifted away. The sun was low now and the late-afternoon air chilly. Beano saw Principal Tyler and Mr. Custer standing at the sideline. He waved and said to himself, "Where were you when I needed you?"

Then he saw the person he was seeking hurrying toward him—Mr. Bagley.

The newsman spoke first, and the words came out in a rush. "What was that business at the end? Are you trying to put in a new formation? If you do, Coach Pritchard will get off his hospital bed and come after you. You'd better remember—"

"It's a fake punt, that's all," Beano said. "And I want to talk to you about it."

As they walked toward the school building, Beano explained Coach Morse's suggestion.

When they passed Principal Tyler and Mr. Custer, the principal called out, "How'd it go today?"

"Fine, fine," Beano called back.

Beano turned back to Mr. Bagley. "What I want to ask is, well, will you promise not to write anything in the paper about it? The only chance of a fake punt working is if we're able to surprise them."

Mr. Bagley nodded his understanding. He turned without speaking and gave Beano a strange look for a long moment. Then he said, "All right, sure."

That evening, when Beano's father called from St. Louis, it was Jeremy who answered the phone. There was no doubt who was calling after Jeremy opened by exclaiming, "Beano's coaching the Tigers!"

Beano stepped across and said, "Let me talk to him."

"What was that?" his father asked.

Beano related everything that had happened—Coach Pritchard's accident, Principal Tyler's summons of Beano to his office, the first couple of practice sessions.

There was a long moment of stunned silence. Then his father said, "That's great. I know you'll be able to do it."

Beano nodded unconsciously. His father always supported his efforts and applauded his achievements. "Well, yeah, it's gone okay so far."

"And it'll continue to go okay, I'm sure. You know your football and you know the players.

How are the players taking it? I'll bet everyone was really surprised."

"I can tell you *I* was. Yeah, everyone was real surprised. The players seem okay. But Marty and some of them aren't real sure."

"They'll be okay. It just takes a little time to get used to the idea. You know, get over the shock."

"Uh-huh."

"Hang in there, Coach Hatton."

"Will you be home for the game?"

"You bet I will. I wouldn't miss this for the world. Now let me talk to the mother of the coach of the Barton High Tigers, will you?"

At ten o'clock Beano, with his mother and Jeremy, sat in front of the television set and watched himself walk across the practice field and tell the camera crews why they could not shoot footage of his team's practice.

"You handled that well," his mother said.

"Gee whiz!" an impressed Jeremy exclaimed. "Beano on television!"

Beano marveled at how small he appeared standing in the midst of the television crews.

Chapter 8

Practice the next day started off badly and got worse.

The players were barely on the field when dark clouds blew in and the wind picked up. The people who were scattered around the edge of the field to watch practice took one look at the menacing clouds and left. Truly, the sky seemed ready to open up a torrent of rain. The players, just beginning their preliminary bending and stretching, glanced at the sky and looked questioningly at Beano.

"Keep going," he said. "A little rain never hurt anyone."

Beano remembered the days that Coach Pritchard kept the team on the practice field in the rain. He always said, "Football games are played in all kinds of weather, and so football teams practice in all kinds of weather."

Watching the darkening sky, Beano jogged back to the school building and got himself one of the ponchos the players wore on the sidelines during games when it was raining.

Returning, he reviewed his plan for a full-speed, contact scrimmage. That always was the order of the day for Wednesday in the practice week. And this was Wednesday. Besides, the Tigers needed the tough game-condition work using three linebackers instead of two, and sending Marty racing around end from punt formation. New plays needed more work than just going through the motions.

But rain would mean a slippery playing field— and increased chance of injury.

Beano gave the threatening skies another look. Not a drop of rain had fallen. Not yet, anyway. But maybe none would. The strong winds might blow the black clouds away before they could let loose the rain.

Suddenly Marty Tucker was at Beano's side. "You're not considering a scrimmage, are you?" he asked, leaning in close. "In this weather?"

Startled, Beano turned. He looked at Marty,

then at the players lined up in the end zone. Leaderless, some had stopped the loosening-up exercises.

Beano stared at Marty. He started to point out that there was no rain so far. But then he changed his mind. Beano was not about to discuss a practice decision with the quarterback. Making the decision was the coach's job, not a player's. Marty was just giving him another challenge—sensible or sense-less, it seemed not to matter—and Beano chose to ignore the challenge. So he said, "Please get back to your position leading the calisthenics."

Marty glared at Beano.

"Now," Beano added.

Marty's eyes flashed anger. Beano returned his gaze. Then Marty turned and went back to his post in front of the rows of players.

Beano watched him go, and consciously avoid-ed looking at the players. He knew they were watching him.

Silently Beano let three words drift through his mind: Wednesday, Thursday, Friday. Then three more words: One, two, three. He had to keep the lid on for three days, from now through the game. He was not sure he could do it.

Already, through Todd, Marty had tried to take over the offensive unit's practice schedule and the game's play calling. He had objected to the plan to run from punt formation, despite the fact—or so Beano thought—that Marty saw the prospects of scoring on a long run. It was a protest against Beano more than an objection to the play. Now he was questioning a scrimmage before the rain began to fall.

Even off the practice field, in the corridors of Barton High, Beano saw signs of trouble. Twice during the day, Beano's sudden appearance had stopped Marty in mid-sentence. Beano had no idea what Marty was saying, but his sudden halt was a sure indication his remarks involved the acting head coach.

No question, he was sure, the quarterback's resentment at having the skinny, bespectacled student manager acting like he was the coach of the Tigers was not subsiding. It was growing.

With a final look at the black clouds, Beano stepped forward and called out: "All right, all right. Let's go! Full-speed scrimmage. First-team offense against first-team defense."

Somebody said, "Beano, it's going to rain."

Beano ignored the remark.

Marty appeared in front of him again and said, "Can't you see? The bottom is going to fall out any minute." He stared at Beano and added, "We ought to go inside, where we can work on plays."

Beano looked at the sky, then back at Marty. "Can't *you* see?" he repeated Marty's words back at him. "It's not raining."

With that, Beano turned his back on the quarterback and sought out Larry Slider.

"Sometimes three linebackers, sometimes two, okay?" he said to the towering player.

Larry nodded and said nothing.

Beano marched with a ball to the middle of the forty-yard line and placed it on the ground. "Okay, let's go."

For forty-five minutes the Tigers ran and tackled and blocked and passed. Twice, large but scattered raindrops splattered down briefly. Each time they did, Marty stopped, turned, and stared at Beano with an exaggerated look of exasperation on his face.

The second time it happened, Beano said to him, "Marty, that was a raindrop, not a rainfall."

Somebody laughed at his crack, which did not help, and Beano instantly regretted saying it.

At the finish Beano called out—"Okay, wind sprints, and go on in. You've earned it."

He stepped back toward the sideline and watched the players move into their wind sprints—all but one.

Marty turned and jogged off the field, toward the school building. It was a defiant gesture, Beano knew. His first instinct was to shout for him to return, to demand that he come back and run his wind sprints with the other players. But Beano did not do it. He stood silently and watched as Marty reached the door, pulled it open, and went in without looking back.

Beano turned to the players running up and down the field. A lot of them were looking around at him as they ran, which meant they had seen Marty leave the field and go in. They were watching for Beano's reaction.

Beano stood motionless and expressionless, staring at nothing somewhere across the field. Then the players, one by one, finished their runs, peeled off, and jogged past him toward the school building. Beano followed the last ones through the door and into the corridor leading to the dressing room.

As he walked toward the dressing-room door, Beano realized that he did not know what to do. For sure, he knew what Coach Pritchard would do—send Marty back onto the field to run his wind sprints. And Marty would do it or leave the team.

But Beano knew that throwing the quarterback off the team would be a mark of failure, not success, on his part. Yet he knew equally well that he could not afford to let Marty get away with this latest challenge.

Pushing through the door to the dressing room, Beano still did not know how he was going to handle the situation, nor even what he was going to face in the dressing room.

Beano heard Marty's voice as he stepped through the door, and he understood Marty's words, and he knew instantly that Marty himself was providing the answer.

Marty was already dressed in his street clothes. He must have skipped his shower in his haste. He was standing in the midst of several dirt-streaked players, none of whom had made the first move toward undressing for the showers.

"I'm not taking orders from that little squirt," Marty was announcing. "You can do what you want, but I'm through."

Beano stopped, and all the faces in the dressing room turned toward him.

Marty actually grinned at Beano, but his eyes were flashing anger.

The dressing room was silent. Beano was sure he could hear his heart pounding—there was a distinct *thumpa-thumpa-thumpa*—and probably, he figured, everyone in the dressing room could hear it as well. How could they help it?

Then Beano spoke. "If you're quitting the team, Marty, please leave the dressing room."

Again silence, except for the beating of Beano's heart.

Marty's expression changed. The look of anger gave way to a look of surprise. Then the anger returned. "You bet," he said. "Gladly."

Beano stepped aside to let Marty walk past him. Marty left the door open in his wake.

Beano stepped across, closed the door, and turned back to the staring players. He started to say *Anyone else who wants to quit, you can leave now,* but he didn't. Instead he looked around the room in silence. To his surprise, he seemed to have his beating heart under control.

Then he found the face in the crowd that he was looking for. He stared into Todd Bowman's eyes. Was Marty's best friend, and the Tigers' running back, going to walk out too?

Todd gave a little shake of his head in reply to Beano's unspoken question.

Nobody else moved or spoke.

"Okay then," Beano said. He took a deep breath. "Better take your showers. We don't want anyone coming down with a cold before Friday night."

The players shuffled toward their lockers and began pulling dirty sweatshirts over their heads and unstrapping shoulder pads.

Beano watched a minute. Then he turned and opened the door and stepped out of the dressing room into the corridor, pulling the door closed behind him. He stood for a moment, luxuriating in being alone, without the eyes of a single person on him. From the gymnasium Beano heard the sounds of the basketball team at practice.

Then Beano gave a little shrug, turned, and headed for the staircase leading up to the main floor.

The staircase was empty of people and shadowy in the gloom of the cloudy afternoon. The corridor on the main floor was empty too, but lights were on in the lobby.

Beano walked down the corridor, across the lobby, and into the school office.

Mrs. Busby, who ran the office, looked up as Beano entered. She smiled at him.

"Principal Tyler?" Beano asked.

"Yes, Beano. Go on in."

Beano walked through the open door to the principal's office. Ed Tyler looked up from his desk and asked, "What's wrong, Beano?"

The abrupt question surprised him. Beano was always reading other people's faces, trying to find indications of their thoughts. But it had never dawned on him that his face too might reveal what was in his mind.

"Sit down," Principal Tyler said without waiting for Beano to answer his question.

Beano sat on a chair opposite the principal's desk. "Marty Tucker has quit the team, and I thought you should hear it first from me," he said.

"Marty? He's quit? Why?"

Beano said, "I think he doesn't like the coach."

"What happened?"

Beano wondered how deeply he should delve into the short history of Marty Tucker, quarterback, and Beano Hatton, acting coach. Not deeply at all, Beano decided, and related only the happenings of the afternoon on the practice field.

Principal Tyler listened without speaking and sat silent for a moment after Beano had finished. Then he said, "Do you want me to have a talk with Marty?"

"No."

Beano's single word hung there in the silence for a moment.

Then Principal Tyler repeated the word with

a question mark. "No? That's all, just—no?"

Beano leaned forward. "Coach Pritchard always said that no single player is more important than the team. The team is going to play Carterville on Friday night. If Marty doesn't want to be on the team, that's his business. The team is still going to play." He paused. "Coach Pritchard would not in a million years ask Marty to come back."

Principal Tyler watched Beano. Then he said, "All right."

Beano got to his feet. "I've got to get back to the dressing room," he said. "I want to have a talk with Dave Harris before he leaves for home about being our quarterback."

Chapter 9

Walking home in the darkness, Beano felt a twinge of something very strange. Reluctantly he finally allowed himself to identify the feeling as self-doubt. For Beano Hatton, self-doubt was a rare visitor. Beano Hatton almost always knew exactly what he was doing, and why.

But now he felt himself wondering.

Beano had no doubts at all about the wisdom of going ahead with the scrimmage. The Tigers had needed the scrimmage. The dark clouds had threatened rain, but no rain had been falling, and very little rain did fall during the forty-five-minute drill. Marty's objection was groundless, nothing more than defiance, a challenge to Beano's authority.

But as Beano mentally relived the events of the

 91

afternoon, he wondered if he had made the right moves.

When Marty left the field without taking his wind sprints, Beano might have followed him inside, talked to him, and either put things right or perhaps staved off the crisis. Should he have done that? No.

And when Marty walked out of the dressing room after having announced that he was quitting, Beano might have left the dressing room behind him, caught him in the corridor, urged him to reconsider. Should he have given that a try? No.

With a nod of his head, Beano could have given approval to Principal Tyler's suggestion of talking to Marty. Might that have worked? Probably not.

But as the questions and answers bounced through Beano's mind, there always was the tougher question that gave rise to his doubts: Was what I did best for the team?

For sure, the Barton High Tigers' chances against the Carterville Bobcats were sharply diminished without Marty Tucker playing quarterback.

But then, the brief meeting with Dave Harris in the dressing room had gone better than Beano had hoped.

Dave, a sophomore, seemed more excited than frightened by the prospect of playing. Beano had feared that when he returned to the dressing room, he would find Dave, who hadn't run more than six plays all season, a nervous wreck at having suddenly been thrust into the spotlight.

But as he listened to Beano, Dave was full of promises he kept repeating: "I'll do my best" and "I can do it, don't worry."

Well, maybe, Beano concluded. Maybe Dave could do it. Beano had no idea how good the substitute might—or might not—be.

As Beano stepped onto his front porch, the skies finally let loose their torrent of rain. He turned and watched the downpour in the darkness for a moment. "Thanks for waiting," he said aloud. Some things, at least, were working out the right way.

Inside, his mother greeted him with: "Has Marty Tucker really quit the team?"

Beano blinked at her. Where had she heard about it? So he asked her, "Where in the world did you hear about it?"

"John Bagley called from the *Chronicle*. He said that Marty was telling everyone around town that he'd quit. Mr. Bagley wants you to call him."

Beano sighed, dropped his books on a chair, and slipped out of his jacket.

"You'll have to hurry," she said. "Dinner is almost on the table."

Jeremy popped into the room, a stricken look on his face. "Isn't Marty going to play for you?"

"It doesn't look that way."

"But Marty's the quarterback."

"Not anymore, it seems. Look, I've got to make a telephone call."

Jeremy watched as Beano found the number of the *Chronicle* and dialed.

Mr. Bagley came on the line with a question: "Is it true that Marty quit the team?"

"Yes, it's true."

There was a moment of silence on the line, as if Mr. Bagley needed time to digest the confirmation. Then he asked, "What happened?"

Beano frowned and did not answer immediately. He knew his words were probably going to appear in print. He wanted them to be the right words. But what were the right words?

Finally he said, "At the end of practice today, Marty refused to take his wind sprints and went into the dressing room. When I got there, he had dressed. He announced he was quitting and left the dressing room."

"But . . . "

Beano did not speak into the silence left by Mr. Bagley.

"But Beano, why?"

"You'll have to ask him about his reasons, Mr. Bagley."

"I will." He paused. "Had there been any trouble earlier?"

Beano hesitated. Then he said, "I had no indication that he was going to quit."

"I see."

Beano wondered what Mr. Bagley meant by that, but he did not ask.

"So," Mr. Bagley continued, "you'll be playing Dave Harris at quarterback against Carterville?"

"It looks that way."

"Does Mr. Tyler know that Marty has quit the team?"

"Yes. I told him."

"What did he say?"

"You'll have to talk to Principal Tyler to get his comments."

"Okay, okay. This is bad news."

"Yes, it is."

Finally Beano was able to hang up.

He got through his dinner and an hour of his studies before Todd Bowman called.

"Look," Todd said, his voice taking on a soft-sounding, confidential tone, "I think Marty will come back if you ask him in the right way."

Beano couldn't help asking, "The right way?"

"Yeah, you know."

"No, I don't know."

The line was silent a moment. Then Todd said, "I've been talking to him. I think Marty is already sorry he walked out."

Beano wanted to ask if Marty was there with Todd, listening in on the conversation. But he didn't.

After the pause that Beano let pass without speaking, Todd said, "Marty's father has been all over him ever since he heard about it—quitting, I mean."

For what it was worth, Todd's mention of Marty's father seemed to confirm that Marty wasn't listening in on the conversation. This pleased Beano. He felt that he was really having a conversation with Todd instead of being the target of some sort of scheme to get Marty reinstated.

Beano said, "Marty is free to come back."

"Will you tell him that?"

"He already knows it. And if he doesn't, you can tell him."

"Oh, c'mon, Beano, you can't expect Marty to come crawling back to you."

"No, I don't expect that. But it's up to him whether he plays. It's his decision, not mine. He knows he can come back to the team, so it's up to him whether he does or doesn't."

"Umm," Todd said. "Will you talk to him about it?"

"Sure."

"Okay. Will you call him right now?"

Beano almost grinned into the telephone. "No, I won't call him. I'm not going to ask him to come back."

"But you said—"

"I said that I'll talk to him, and I will—any time he wants to talk. Look, Marty announced he was quitting by telling me, and he can come back by telling me. But I'm not going to ask him."

Todd gave up, and they said good-bye. And for the rest of the evening, Beano half expected the telephone to ring. But it didn't.

Thursday morning Beano pulled open the front door of the school building and stepped into the lobby just a couple of minutes ahead of the first bell. The rush of warm air inside the building felt good after the long walk in the dry and frosty morning air that had moved in behind the night-long rain.

Knowing that all eyes were on him, Beano

avoided looking around the lobby as he turned right and headed for his classroom.

Suddenly Mr. Custer was standing in front of him. "I was hoping you would call me last night," he said.

"Huh?"

"Sometimes it helps just to talk a problem through."

Beano managed a small smile. "Oh, I had a chance to talk—first to Mr. Bagley, then to Todd Bowman."

"Has anything changed?"

"Not that I know of."

The first bell clanged.

"Come see me if I can do anything," Mr. Custer said.

"Thanks. I will."

Beano walked on down the corridor. He was drawing curious stares. Clearly everyone at Barton High already knew that the quarterback had walked out on the acting coach. So how was Beano taking it? Well, everyone was gawking, trying to find out.

Oddly, Beano didn't see any of the football players in the stream of students in the corridor. Usually they hung around in the lobby before the first class and then walked in groups to class when the bell rang. But there were none in sight. Strange.

Beano walked on, trying to wear his everything-is-coming-up-roses expression.

As he turned into the classroom—Mrs. Harrison's physics class—someone in the corridor called out, "Beano! Hang in there!"

He turned. Several students grinned and waved at him. He could not determine which of them had shouted the encouragement.

Beano was sitting at Coach Pritchard's desk during his third-period study hall, working on the practice plan and his game plan when Principal Tyler appeared in the door. "Anything new?" he asked.

"Not that I know of," Beano said, idly wondering how many times he had spoken those five words.

Then Principal Tyler said that Coach Pritchard was able to have an occasional visitor and had asked to see Beano. "He knows you're coaching the Tigers against Carterville," he said.

"Oh?"

"We'll go after practice."

"Okay, fine."

"And we won't mention the Marty Tucker matter."

"Sure."

During the day, Beano saw Marty twice, once walking with Todd and a couple of other players, and once alone coming out of a classroom. On both occasions Beano nodded a greeting as if nothing existed between them and Marty nodded back. It was the same as back in the days when Marty acted as if he didn't know Beano Hatton existed.

Beano encountered Dave Harris once, in the cafeteria during the lunch period. Dave was laughing and joking with some friends. He looked the picture of a guy on top of the world. And why not? He was going to be the starting quarterback on Friday night. Beano waved at Dave and grinned as he passed, hoping that Dave would be as happy after the game as he was now.

And one other time during the day somebody shouted: "Beano! Hang in there!"

A half-dozen players were in the dressing room when Beano arrived. He went to the training table and dumped his books, then pulled out the clipboard bearing the practice plan.

Todd Bowman entered behind him, and Beano said, as matter-of-factly as possible, "Todd, will you lead them in the warm-up calisthenics?"

Todd blinked, as if realizing for the first time that Marty Tucker, who usually led the warm-up exercises, was not going to be there.

Beano returned Todd's gaze. Did Todd understand that he wanted him out front leading the exercises as visible evidence that Marty Tucker's best friend was still on the team? Probably so, Beano thought.

Todd said, "Yeah, sure," and moved on toward his locker.

Then Beano perched himself on the training table and watched the players enter the room and walk to their lockers and begin to change for practice. What would Beano say if the door opened and Marty Tucker walked in? Nothing, nothing at all.

But Marty did not come through the door.

As Beano sat on the training table, the fact dawned slowly that something in the attitude of the dressing room was different, strange, unusual. The room was quieter than usual. Even Edwin Deere was behaving in a subdued manner. The players seemed to be changing clothes more slowly than usual. Those who were dressed for practice were dawdling with a shoestring or something, instead of leaving for the field.

With an effort Beano maintained his pose on the training table, waiting. Then Beano realized that everyone was looking at Art Fleming, the lanky right end.

As for Art, he looked uncertain, glancing nervously around the room.

Somebody whispered, "Go on."

Art took a deep breath. "Beano," he said. "Some of us had a meeting this morning. Before first period. In the cafeteria."

Beano watched Art and waited.

Art shifted his weight from one foot to the other. "Well Beano, we decided that we're going to beat Carterville—with or without Marty."

Beano was frowning now, unsure about whether his brain should believe what his ears were hearing.

Art shifted his weight again. "Marty's been our quarterback," he said. "But if Marty chooses not to play, well, Dave is our quarterback, and we'll win with Dave."

Art relaxed, an obvious signal that the speech was ended.

Beano looked at the players around him, then back at Art. He smiled, nodded, raised a thin arm with a fist at the end of it, and said, "All right!"

Now, he thought, if we can just convince the Carterville Bobcats.

Chapter 10

Beano headed the Tigers into a light signal drill, the usual routine for a Thursday. Whatever might be gained by hard tackling and blocking was more than lost if players turned out for the game on Friday night with painful bruises and aching muscles. The hard work was over by Thursday, and the practice was devoted to putting the finishing touches on the offense and the defense.

For him, though, this Thursday practice was more—much more—than the usual light signal drill.

The Tigers suddenly had a new and untried quarterback. The running backs were not accustomed to taking handoffs from Dave Harris. The receivers did not know how his passes arrived. The linemen were unfamiliar with his cadence in calling the signals. And, of course, no one knew the extent—or limits—of Dave Harris's abilities. Everyone had to try to pack a full season of practice, playing, and learning into an hour and a half on the practice field with a new quarterback at the helm.

After the warm-up calisthenics, Beano sent the defensive unit off to the far end of the field with instructions to Larry Slider, the senior linebacker, to take charge and keep them working. Beano was going to be concentrating on an offensive unit trying to adjust to a new quarterback.

Beano got the players lined up and, standing just behind and to the right of the backfield, called a rapid sequence of plays—a handoff into the line, a pitchout to the right, a pass, a quarterback sneak, a quarterback option—and then variations on the plays, over and over again.

Beano was determined to run as many plays as possible in the practice time left to him. Every play revealed something about Dave's strengths and weaknesses to one or more of his teammates. And the more they knew, the better.

Dave was not as strong a runner as Marty, but he was shiftier. His short passes lacked the authority of Marty's bullets, but they were on target more than Beano had dared hope. His handoffs and his pitchouts were of a different texture than Marty's, which was to be expected. But they worked.

Gradually, in the quick repetition of the plays, the backs and the linemen working with Dave seemed to Beano to be fitting into the new pattern. Their confidence in the new quarterback was growing with every play.

Art Fleming served as Dave's self-appointed cheerleader, calling out, "Good pass!" every time he pulled in a throw over center or a toss into the flat.

To Beano's surprise, Todd Bowman stopped the play once to suggest to Dave that his pitchouts needed more spin. "A dead ball is heavy, tougher to catch," he said. Dave nodded his thanks, and his pitchouts had more zip to them after that.

Maybe, Beano thought as he watched from his vantage point at the edge of the backfield, just maybe the Tigers could win with Dave at quarterback. This just might work. Aloud, he said, "Run it again, same play."

The crowd of onlookers along the sidelines had been curiously quiet in the opening minutes of the drill. Everyone in town knew by now about Marty quitting, and a lot of them had come out to see—and judge—for themselves the Tigers' new quarterback. As the drill moved along, and Dave clearly was looking better than anyone had expected, the crowd livened up. There were occasional shouts of "Go, Dave!" and "Way to go!"

Then Dave silenced the crowd with his first long pass.

Beano had called the play with almost a shrug of the shoulders. All the previous plays had been standard, conservative plays—handoffs, pitchouts, short passes—the safe stuff for an untried quarterback.

When he called the play that sent Art Fleming and Joe Burgess deep downfield, with Dave backtracking without a fake and then throwing, Beano figured he was going to see a high wobbler of a pass fall to the ground or, as with Marty's long throws, a wildly inaccurate shot—with either of them having interception written all over it.

But Dave took the snap, backpedaled quickly, looked, cocked his arm, and fired the ball thirty-five yards on a clothesline to Art.

After a moment of awed silence, someone in the crowd at the sidelines let out a long, low whistle.

Beano watched the trajectory of the pass, saw Art reach out and pull in the ball without breaking stride, and turned and blinked at Dave. "Do that again, will you?" he said.

Dave smiled and did it again, this time hitting Joe.

Now Beano was smiling. Dave Harris may not be the quarterback that Marty was. He did not have the strength or the experience. But he did bring to the Tigers an unexpected and powerful weapon.

Because of Marty's inaccuracy with the long throw, Coach Pritchard seldom bothered to practice the few long downfield passes in the Tigers' playbook and never allowed one to find its way into his conservative game plans. And Dave, playing second string behind Marty, practiced the same system. Surely Coach Pritchard was aware of Dave's ability, but Marty was the starting quarterback. Until now, that is.

There were shouts and whoops for Dave from the sidelines crowd as Beano called the next series of plays.

Beano kept his concentration on the players on the field until he heard, in the unmistakable high-pitched tone of Jeremy, "Hey, Beano!"

Beano glanced in the direction of the shout. He spotted his little brother and waved.

And beyond Jeremy, a half a block away across

the gravel parking lot, Beano saw Marty Tucker walking along the street, his face turned toward the practice field.

For a moment Beano stared. Marty, coming out of the school building, had swung wide to avoid walking past the field where all the players and onlookers were sure to spot him. Beano's first thought was that Marty was heading for home instead of practicing with the basketball team. The thought surprised him. Marty obviously had not joined the basketball team today. But why was he so late in leaving school? Maybe, Beano thought, he had spoken to Coach Beardsley after school and would be joining the basketball team tomorrow. Yes, that must be it.

Then Marty, as if sensing that Beano had spotted him, turned his back to the field and walked on.

"Quarterback option to the right," Beano called out to the players.

At the end of the drill, Beano was walking toward the school building behind the last of the players when he came upon Todd Bowman.

Todd was clearly waiting for him, and Beano approached him with a questioning look on his face. As he drew near, he said, "Yes?"

"Beano, who's going to do our punting?"

Marty Tucker was the Tigers' punter. But Marty Tucker had quit the team.

Beano looked at the sky. He wanted to slap himself on the forehead. Todd's question was a good one. Yes, who?

Beano turned to Todd. "Can you punt?"

"I guess so."

"Okay, you're it."

Todd smiled and shrugged. "Okay," he said.

Then Beano said, "I hope you were watching when we had Marty trying the run from punt formation."

"Yeah."

The two of them walked on into the building with Beano wondering what else he might have forgotten.

When the last player had left the dressing room, Beano scooped up his books and headed upstairs to Principal Tyler's office for the hospital visit with Coach Pritchard.

Principal Tyler was at his desk, in his shirtsleeves, studying a computer printout. He looked up when Beano appeared in his office door. "I'll be about fifteen more minutes," he said, glancing at his wristwatch. "Our appointment at the hospital is at six. It's outside the regular visiting hours, you know. No reason to arrive early. Have a seat out there, will you, and I'll be right with you." Then he added, "How was practice?"

"Oh, fine."

"Is Dave all right? He's been thrown into the starting role pretty suddenly."

"He's fine."

"Good."

Principal Tyler turned his gaze back to the computer printout, and Beano started back out the door toward a chair in the outer office.

"Oh, Beano," Principal Tyler said.

Beano stopped and turned back to the principal.

"You did tell your mother, didn't you, that you were going to be late this evening?"

Beano smiled. "Yes, I called her from Coach Pritchard's office after you told me this morning."

Principal Tyler nodded and turned his attention back to the computer printout.

Beano took a seat on one of the straight wooden chairs lined up against the wall with a low table in front.

When he put his books on the table, he noticed a copy of the Barton *Chronicle*. He picked it up almost tentatively, not sure he really wanted to turn to the sports page and read what John Bagley had written about the Tigers. He glanced at the front page. Unemployment was down. Protestors were in the streets somewhere in Europe. The city council was still arguing about parking meters.

He took a breath and opened to the sports page.

The headline read: MARTY TUCKER QUITS TIGERS.

The subhead read: *Dave Harris to Start at QB Against Carterville.*

Beano read on. The quotations attributed to him were, as well as he could remember, accurate. But he was less interested in his own quotes than in those of Marty Tucker. What had Marty said to John Bagley?

Beano scanned the printed words until he saw Marty's name. Then he leaned forward, frowned, and read. Marty was quoted as saying, "If Beano Hatton thinks he knows more about football than I do, then let him do it without me. I am not going to take orders on the field from the student manager."

Beano, his frown deepening, looked up and found himself staring into the face of Principal Tyler. He had his suit jacket on now, and his overcoat was draped across his arm.

"Reading about the Tigers?" he asked.

"Yes."

"I think Marty may already regret those remarks—and may be regretting that he quit, too."

Beano nodded.

"Things may work themselves out before the game tomorrow night," Principal Tyler said. "C'mon, let's go."

Beano got to his feet, wondering if Marty's late departure from school may have been caused by a meeting with Principal Tyler. But he didn't ask.

Beano had been in a hospital only once before. He had visited Denny Overman when his friend had had his appendix removed. Beano had not liked the hospital. It smelled different from any place he had ever been before. It looked too clean to be comfortable. And the quiet of the place was, well, spooky. He hoped he never had to be hospitalized.

Following Principal Tyler and a nurse down the corridor toward Coach Pritchard's room, Beano noticed that the smell was the same, the too-clean look was the same, and the quiet was the same.

The nurse stopped outside a door and said to Principal Tyler, "Just a few minutes, please."

"Yes, of course," Principal Tyler said, and he and Beano walked into the room.

Coach Pritchard was on his back with the head of the high bed raised slightly. He wore two bandages on his head. His right arm was in a cast. And his right leg, in a cast, was suspended just above the bed by a line going up to a pulley at the ceiling. He had a deep bruise on his face. And his skin seemed sort of gray, but maybe that was because of the light in the room.

Coach Pritchard said to Beano, "How's it going, coach?" He smiled slightly and then, as if it hurt, turned off the smile.

"Okay," Beano said. "We're going to beat Carterville for you."

"That's what I wanted to hear."

Beano nodded. He didn't know what to do next. So he said, "Everyone has been really worried about you."

"Oh, they say I'm going to be all right. But it's going to take a little time."

"That's all right."

"I've been reading about you in the *Chronicle*. Sounds like you've got everything under control." He looked at Principal Tyler and said, "But the *Chronicle* wasn't delivered today."

Beano kept his gaze straight ahead and decided to let Principal Tyler field that one.

"I'll bring you a copy when I visit on Saturday," Principal Tyler said.

Coach Pritchard looked at Beano. "The nurse is

going to run you two out of here in just a few minutes. But I wanted to see you, Beano. I wanted to tell you that it was a relief when I learned that you were taking over in my absence. I have every confidence in you. I want you to remember that tomorrow night during the game. You'll make all the right moves. I'm sure of that, and I wanted you to know."

Beano nodded, not daring to try to speak. He was afraid he was going to choke up. When he could, he said again, "We're going to beat Carterville for you."

"Win or lose," Coach Pritchard said, "I'm proud of all of you, and I want you to tell the team that for me. Will you do it?"

"Sure."

As if on cue, the nurse appeared in the door. She did not speak.

"I told you she was going to run you out of here, didn't I?" Coach Pritchard said. He again gave a little smile, then quit the effort quickly.

Beano noticed the car parked in front of the house next door when Principal Tyler pulled up to the curb to let Beano out. But he thought nothing of it.

"See you tomorrow," Principal Tyler said as Beano opened the car door.

"Yes, right," he said.

Beano, his books gathered up under his left arm, stepped out of the car and closed the door. He stood a moment watching Principal Tyler's car move away in the darkness.

Then he heard two car doors slam—the car parked in front of the house next door—and a voice calling his name.

He turned and stared into the darkness.

"Beano, it's me, Todd; and I've got Marty with me."

Chapter 11

They were approaching Beano in the darkness.

Beano walked forward to meet them.

"We've been waiting," Todd said. "Your mother told us you were going to the hospital to see Coach Pritchard. We decided to wait in the car instead of coming back later."

Beano waited. Then, when neither Todd nor Marty spoke, he said, "Uh-huh,"—and waited again. He wished he could see their faces better in the darkness.

Todd broke the silence. "How's Coach Pritchard?"

Beano, squinting at Marty in the shadows and remembering the near sneer on his face when he walked out just over twenty-four hours ago, turned to Todd. Reasonable as it was, the question surprised him. Beano thought they would want to get down to the purpose of their visit right away.

"Coach Pritchard?" Beano repeated. "Oh, he looked pretty banged up, but he seemed in good spirits. He said he was sure that everything is going to be okay."

"That's good," Todd said.

Beano looked back at Marty.

Marty spoke, "Did you tell him that I . . . ?"

"No."

"But he must know. He would have heard from someone, or would have seen the *Chronicle*."

"No, he doesn't know what's happened. I think they must have kept the *Chronicle* away from him. He said they told him the paper hadn't been delivered to the hospital today."

Todd took over. "That's good that he doesn't know, because it's all fixed now anyway. Marty wants to come back to the team. He wants to play tomorrow night. Right, Marty?"

Before Marty could answer, Beano said, "C'mon in the house. I'm freezing out here. We can talk inside."

Beano was interested in more than warmth. He wanted to be able to see Marty's face. If Marty came back at this point, it had to be on Beano's terms. And Beano had to see Marty's face in order to try and read his thoughts.

"Aw, I don't know," Marty said.

"Your mother will be there and everything," Todd added.

"She won't bother us," Beano said, "and I can chase Jeremy away."

"Jeremy?" Marty asked.

"My little brother."

Todd and Marty glanced at each other. Beano thought that Todd was acting as if he wanted to get the matter settled as quickly as possible. And Marty? It seemed to Beano that Marty was acting as if he was confident of reinstatement and simply wanted the whole uncomfortable session over as quickly as possible.

"C'mon," Beano said with a tone of finality, and turned and walked toward his house.

Todd and Marty followed him.

Beano held open the front door for them and then walked in himself. He gestured at chairs in the empty living room and said, "Have a seat."

He heard the television from the den and knew that Jeremy was in there. He walked toward the kitchen and met his mother coming out.

She said, "Marty Tucker and Todd Bowman were—oh, I see they're with you."

Mrs. Hatton glanced at Marty and Todd, still

standing in the living room and smiled at them—
then at Beano—and left without another word.

When Beano rejoined Marty and Todd in the
living room, he saw Jeremy's head poking out
through the door to the den.

"Just get back to your program," Beano said to
him.

Jeremy's head disappeared from the doorway.

"Have a seat," Beano told Marty and Todd
again, slipping out of his jacket and draping it over
the back of a chair.

The two players sat down without taking off
their jackets. Both clearly were hoping that this
wasn't going to take long and that they would
quickly be on their way.

Beano sat in the chair where his jacket was
hung and looked at Marty. He said, "Well?"

Marty crossed his legs, then uncrossed them.
There was nothing near to a sneer on his face this
time. He looked decidedly uncomfortable. Clearly
Marty Tucker had had little experience with repen-
tance. Beano was sure of that. Marty Tucker starred
as quarterback on the football team, and he starred
at forward on the basketball team. Marty Tucker
never had to ask for favors, never had to apologize.

Todd leaned in. "It's like I said—"

Beano gave Todd a look that stopped him in

mid-sentence. "I'd like to hear it from Marty," he said, "because we're going to have to work together in a game tomorrow night." He took a breath and continued, speaking slowly and softly. "I'm going to have to be convinced in my own mind that we can do that: work together in a game."

Marty's eyes flashed anger for a moment, but he forced a small smile. "You make it kind of tough, don't you, Beano?"

Beano watched Marty without changing expression. Then he said, "I don't want to have to disagree with the quarterback in front of a bleacherful of people tomorrow night."

Marty nodded, and seemed to be framing words in his mind. "I want to come back, and I want to play tomorrow night."

That's not enough, Beano thought, but said nothing. He watched Marty and waited.

"He's a senior—it's his last game," Todd said.

Beano wished he could banish Todd to the den to watch television with Jeremy.

Marty continued as if Todd had not spoken. "Look, I lost my temper yesterday, and I'm sorry. I did something that I regret, and I want to undo it. Let's just put it behind us and go back to where we were. Okay?"

"No," Beano said.

Marty almost flinched at the word. Todd blinked at Beano in astonishment.

"Where we were," Beano said, using Marty's words, "was you challenging me on every point, whether it made sense or not, just for the sake of challenge. And that is what I am not going to have in the game tomorrow night."

Marty eyed Beano and then turned his gaze to a spot on the floor between them.

For once Todd did not interrupt the silence.

"Okay," Marty said finally, with a little nod. "Okay." Then, almost as if speaking to himself, he added, "Everybody has been making me feel like a worm. My father, Coach Beardsley, Mr. Bagley." He looked at Todd and said, "Even Todd." He looked back at Beano. "And some of the other players too."

Beano nodded his head slightly and said nothing. But in his brain one of the names Marty listed stood out. Coach Beardsley. So Marty had tried to go out for basketball and Coach Beardsley had put him down the hard way. Beano gave a silent cheer for Coach Beardsley.

But Marty still had not said what Beano was waiting for, and he intentionally held off welcoming the quarterback's return to the team.

Apparently sensing that more was required,

Marty leaned toward Beano and said, "Look, Beano, you know more about football than I thought you knew when this week started. We can work together in the game. We both want to win the game." He paused, took a breath, and said, "You coach, I'll play."

Beano nodded. That was what he was waiting for. He said, "Right."

Marty looked unsure of the meaning of Beano's response. "You mean—well, we're okay?"

"Yeah, we're okay. On those terms, I can put it behind me if you can put it behind you, and we'll just worry about the game tomorrow night."

Todd leaned back and smiled.

Marty did not thank Beano, and Beano was glad of it.

Beano closed the front door behind Marty and Todd and called out to his mother, "Okay."

Jeremy came out of the den. "Are we going to eat dinner now?"

"Yep."

"That was Marty Tucker."

Beano looked at his younger brother. "Yep," he said.

Beano walked into the kitchen, where his mother was putting food on the table. She stopped and turned to Beano. "Is Marty rejoining the team for the Carterville game?"

"Yes."

"That's good. Now sit down and eat your dinner."

"I've got to give Dave Harris a call," Beano said.

"Not until you've eaten."

Beano took a deep breath and spoke into the telephone. "Dave, Marty is rejoining the team and will be starting the game tomorrow night."

There was a long silence on the telephone line. Then Dave said, "What? I mean, what happened?"

Beano hesitated a moment before answering. Then he chose his words carefully. "Marty came to my house this evening and asked to come back to the team." Beano paused, then said, "I didn't ask him to return, Dave." Again, a pause. "He asked me."

"I see." The words were flat, without feeling.

Beano frowned. This was very unpleasant. "Dave," he said finally, "I was perfectly prepared to play the Carterville game with you at quarterback. But Marty has been the quarterback all season, and this is his last game."

"Sure. I understand."

Beano, remembering the surprising accuracy of Dave's long passes, started to tell Dave that he was sure to see some playing time in the game. But then he decided against it. For sure, Dave might see some playing time. But Beano did not want to make a promise that circumstances might prevent him from keeping.

He replaced the telephone and sat, unmoving, for a moment with his hand still on the receiver. He remembered Dave's excitement and confidence at the prospect of playing. He recalled his wide grins when he connected with those long passes to Art and Joe. And, with a frown, Beano wondered if Coach Pritchard had ever had to let down a player like he'd just done.

Beano then took a deep breath, picked up the telephone directory to look up Principal Tyler's home telephone number, and dialed.

The principal listened while Beano gave an abbreviated account of his meeting with Marty. Then he said, "That's great news, Beano. Great news for the team—and for Marty, too."

"Yes," Beano said, and then added under his breath as he hung up the telephone, "I hope so."

Chapter 12

By the time Beano arrived at Barton High the next morning, everyone in the lobby and the corridors knew that Marty was rejoining the team and would be playing against Carterville.

But it wasn't enough just to know. Everyone wanted to hear from Beano how it had come about.

"He changed his mind, that's all," Beano said over and over again. "And I'm glad he did."

But everyone was asking: Had Beano asked Marty to come back? Or had Marty asked to be allowed to return? What had Marty said? What had Beano said? Was it true that Todd had been there?

One of the rumors circulating was that Coach Pritchard had called Marty from his hospital bed and told him to rejoin the team. Was that true?

Beano grinned at all the questions—and said nothing.

He saw Marty at the center of a crowd of students, mostly members of the football team. He was smiling and talking, and obviously enjoying his role at the center of attention.

As Beano went by, Marty called out, "Hey, Beano."

Beano smiled and waved, joining in the public display that everything was all right now between the acting coach and the quarterback. "Are you ready?" Beano called to him.

"Ready," Marty said.

Everyone watched and listened.

Just before the opening bell rang, Mr. Custer, standing outside the door to his classroom, gestured to Beano, and Beano walked across to him.

"Sometime after the season is over, you'll have to tell me what happened," Mr. Custer said.

Beano grinned at his teacher. "Sure," he said.

Fifteen minutes into the first class, Beano was summoned to Principal Tyler's office.

"This is getting to be a habit," Mrs. Harrison said, smiling. Beano marveled at her words. Was it only four days ago that he had gone to the principal's office from physics class to learn that he was the acting football coach?

Beano nodded to Mrs. Harrison and walked out behind Margaret Young again. Beano was puzzled. Marty was back on the team, so there were no problems. Or were there?

Principal Tyler was waiting for Beano in the doorway to his office. He seemed ruffled. "Most unusual," he said. "But I guess this whole week has been most unusual. Come in, Beano."

Beano followed the principal into his office, still puzzled.

Principal Tyler stopped in the center of his office instead of seating himself at his desk. He pointed to the chair alongside his desk and said, "Sit there." Beano sat down. Then the principal picked up his telephone and placed it on the corner of the desk next to Beano. "Call John Bagley at the *Chronicle*. He's just heard that Marty has rejoined the team. I told him that you were in class, of course. But he's right on deadline and is having a fit because you didn't call him last night. That's the number there, on that piece of paper."

As Beano picked up the piece of paper and began to dial, Principal Tyler said, "And then go back to your class."

"Sure thing," Beano said.

Two classroom periods later, during study hall,

Beano sat at the desk in the coaches' office, determined to create what he hoped was a satisfactory final draft of a game plan for the Tigers against the Carterville Bobcats.

He had never written a game plan before. In fact, he had never even seen a game plan.

But he knew that Coach Pritchard always paced the sidelines at games carrying a clipboard holding a sheaf of papers. Throughout the game, he was always referring to the papers. Beano knew the clipboard held the Tigers' game plan.

Beano wished he could lay his hands on one of Coach Pritchard's old game plans. He could not just copy it, he knew. Each opponent was different, requiring its own game plan. But seeing the form, and what kind of items were listed, would have been a big help.

If he had been thinking, Beano could have asked Coach Pritchard about the game plan when he visited him in the hospital. Perhaps the coach would have given him the key to the desk, or the file cabinet, and told him where to look. But no, Beano realized that he would not have asked for the key, and maybe it would not have been offered.

For a moment Beano considered calling back one of the coaches—Coach Morse of Barrow Mea-

dows High or Coach Patton of Warrington High—
and asking for guidance. They had both been helpful. Maybe they would be helpful again. But then
Beano shook his head. He did not want to impose
on them any further. And, more important, he did
not want to confess his ignorance.

So Beano was left to his own devices.

Beano knew that the game plan was a collec-
tion of plays that might work against a particular
team—with particular strengths and weaknesses—
in a particular set of circumstances on the field.

He glanced through his notes from the telephone conversations with the two coaches, trying
to picture the kind of game the Carterville coach
would be planning.

Then he stared at the legal-size pad of yellow
pages, shrugged, and drew lines dividing the sheet
into three sections. At the head of the top section he
wrote: "General." Okay, he thought, these are the
items I've got to keep in mind from beginning to
end. He wrote a sentence: "Got to make each possession pay off because Carterville, with its strong
ground game, is going to control the ball." He
raised an eyebrow as he reread what he had written. Easier said than done, he thought. Then he
wrote: "Carterville doesn't like to pass . . . try to
make them . . . force long yardage on third down."

Again, easier said than done. He jotted down: "Third linebacker?" Then he wrote, in response to the Bobcats' grinding ground game: "Substitute defense."

The second section was headed: "Plays." He had only two deserving special mention. He wrote: "Fake punt . . . do it early." Then he wrote: "Dave long pass." Two plays seemed a small number. But he knew of nothing else to note.

He headed the third section: "Sequences." Then he quickly jotted down thoughts that might apply to any opponent, but that he needed to remember throughout the game. A line plunge may help set up a successful pass play. A couple of end runs may cause the linebackers to edge out, setting up a plunge into the middle.

Beano scribbled furiously as the thoughts raced through his mind.

Then he sat back, looked at the penciled words, and said aloud to the empty office, "I hope that's enough of a game plan. We'll all know this time tomorrow."

Suddenly the bell rang. Beano got to his feet, clamped the pages in his clipboard, picked up his books, and walked out.

In the corridor he saw Coach Beardsley and Coach Wyandotte approaching.

Beano waved at them and walked up to Coach Beardsley. "I want to thank you," he said.

"Marty told you?" Coach Beardsley asked. He sounded slightly surprised.

Beano thought a moment, then said, "Yes, sort of." He added, "I'm sure that what you said was very important in changing his mind."

"I'm glad it worked out. Especially for Marty's sake. I think he never would have forgiven himself."

"I agree, but he wasn't going to listen to me."

Coach Beardsley nodded. "Good luck tonight."

"Thanks."

Beano walked into the cafeteria at the start of the lunch period and stopped and looked around. He spotted the first person he was looking for—Marty Tucker—at a lunch table with several players. Then he found the second person he was seeking—Dave Harris—with a couple of students at the other end of the same table.

Beano approached Marty and said, "We need to talk, and this is the only chance we're going to have."

Marty said, "Sure, yeah."

"Let's go over there." Beano gestured at an empty table in the corner of the cafeteria.

Marty nodded, got to his feet, said to the others, "See you later," and started carrying his tray across the cafeteria.

Beano did not follow. He walked down to the end of the table and said to Dave, "Can you come over to that table there? We've got some things that you and Marty and I need to discuss."

Dave raised his eyebrows in surprise. "Me?"

Beano smiled at him. "Yes, you."

Dave glanced across at Marty putting his tray down on the table. "Well, sure," he said, and got to his feet. He looked down at his tray and said, "I'm finished," and turned with Beano.

As Beano and Dave walked across the cafeteria, Beano saw Marty, still standing, glaring at him. Clearly the senior first-string quarterback did not like the idea that the sophomore second-string quarterback was invited to the meeting.

Beano did not know whether to frown or smile at Marty's gaping expression. But he knew that at this time a day earlier Dave Harris had been the quarterback. And—who knew?—he might wind up being the quarterback in tonight's game. Besides, Beano hoped that including Dave might compensate a bit for his disappointment.

When the three of them were seated, Marty

resumed eating his lunch, and Dave asked Beano, "Aren't you going to eat?"

"I haven't got time," Beano said. He put the clipboard containing his game-plan notes on the table and said, "I've got some thoughts jotted down here, based on what I know we can do and what I've learned about Carterville."

Marty gave Beano a sharp look but said nothing.

Beano smiled slightly and said, "I hope that what I've done is a game plan. In any case, this is the basis of how we are going to try to move the ball against Carterville."

Marty finished eating. He leaned back and said, "Are you trying to say, Beano, that you will be calling all the plays?"

Beano eyed Marty a moment before answering. Maybe he had already forgotten last night's statement: *"You coach, I'll play."* Or maybe he had not meant it when he said it.

As casually as he could, Beano said, "Not all of them. But I'll call some of the plays, for sure. There will be times when I see things from the sidelines that you can't see on the field." He paused to let the statement sink in.

Marty waited without speaking.

"Also," Beano continued, "there are things I know about the Carterville Bobcats that you don't. I talked to some coaches whose teams played them. And what I learned from them may indicate a certain play at a certain time. When that situation comes up, I will definitely call the play."

Marty leaned toward Beano. "You what? You talked to some coaches . . . ?"

"Yes, sure," Beano said in his best matter-of-fact manner, as if he always called coaches.

Marty stared at Beano, and Beano thought he could see wheels turning in his mind: So that's what led to the fake punt and run. So that's why Beano talked about blitzing linebackers and short passes.

When Marty said nothing, Beano added. "I had to know something about Carterville in order to devise a strategy."

Marty said only, "Yeah."

"But," Beano concluded, "mostly we'll play our standard offense, and you know more about it than I do. That is, you will know better which play to call than I will."

From Beano's right came Dave's voice. "Maybe we'd better go over the game plan."

"Yes," Beano said. He picked up his clipboard. "I'll run down the items, and you two tell me if I'm wrong or if any of it gives you trouble." He looked at Marty. "Okay?"

Marty spoke the word, "Okay."

For the first time ever, Beano stood with the football players on the auditorium stage during the pep rally. Before, he had always assumed that he did not belong on the stage, accepting the cheers, and nobody had ever said, "C'mon up here with us, Beano." He always sat in the audience at pep rallies.

Beano stood, unmoving, absently watching the cheerleaders lead the shouting students through a cheer. His hands hung at his sides awkwardly. He wanted to thrust them in his pockets or, even better, fold his arms over his chest. He was sure that every person in the audience was watching him.

The whole scene certainly did look different from the stage, he thought. There were all those faces staring up at him, and most of them were shouting. At the back of the auditorium, Mr. Custer was standing, leaning against the wall, watching. Did the teacher always stand at the back during the pep rallies? The noise seemed louder than Beano had ever heard at the other rallies. Even the four-piece Barton High pep band sounded different from up on the stage.

Principal Tyler stepped to the podium. The cheerleaders ran off the stage, three to each side. The band fell silent. And gradually the noise from the audience subsided.

The principal began with a somber report on Coach Pritchard's condition—still serious, but improving. Then he recounted the options considered in the wake of the coach's injury, including the possible cancellation of the last game of the season.

"We decided not to cancel the game but to play," he said, "and we asked Hubert Hatton to step in as acting coach."

Beano grinned at the mention of his first name. Principal Tyler used his nickname in private. But in a formal presentation he reverted to Beano's proper name.

Somebody in the audience shouted a correction—"Beano!"

Principal Tyler turned and looked at Beano with a smile, then leaned back into the microphone and said, "Yes, Beano Hatton."

There was a burst of applause from the audience.

After a few minutes Principal Tyler held up his hands to quiet the crowd and said, "Beano will say a few words." He stepped back and Beano walked toward the podium.

Beano looked at all the faces turned toward him. He felt short of breath, and everyone laughed when he looked up at the microphone and then reached out to lower it. He took a deep breath and, unfortunately, exhaled into the microphone, broadcasting the signal of his nervousness.

The audience was quiet.

Beano began speaking. He spoke softly, almost too softly, enunciating each word carefully. "I am not the coach of the Barton High Tigers," he said. "Our coach is in the hospital, seriously injured. We will be playing Carterville without our coach."

He stopped and took in a breath he badly needed. "I know that I speak for each member of the team when I say that all of us will be giving our very best to beat Carterville and show that Coach Pritchard has done such a fine job of coaching that the team is able to carry on in his absence."

He paused again for breath. Then he said, "We are determined to make him proud of us."

Beano looked out over the audience, giving the impression he had more to say.

But he stepped back, turned, and walked back to his place in the line of players.

Chapter 13

His jacket collar turned up against the cold, Beano walked home after the pep rally, the same as every Friday during football season. It was an afternoon off, free of practice, before the game at night.

Coach Pritchard always advised the players to go home, eat a light meal, and rest, maybe even take a nap. He wanted them neither hungry nor overstuffed and as relaxed as possible when they arrived back at the school for the game. Beano was following the same regimen, which was why he wanted to get the strategy talk with Marty and Dave out of the way during the lunch hour.

But for Beano, this Friday was not the same as every Friday during football season.

Not at all.

When Beano stepped through the front doorway of his home, his mother called out from the head of the stairs, "There's a sandwich for you on the table in the kitchen, and there's milk in the refrigerator."

That was the usual procedure too—but Beano knew that this would be about the last normal happening for him on this Friday.

Beano dropped his books on a chair, removed his jacket and dropped it on top of the books, and walked into the kitchen. Having gone without lunch, he was ready for a meal.

He poured himself a glass of milk, replaced the carton in the refrigerator, and sat down at the table.

For a moment he stared across the sandwich and began making a mental list of all the things that could go wrong with his plans. What if Marty tried to run on a fake punt and Carterville was lying back and waiting for him? Did the Carterville linebackers really like to blitz a lot, or would they hang back and intercept Marty's short passes? What if Dave, called upon to throw a long pass, missed his mark and Carterville picked off the ball?

Beyond all that, what if Marty did, after all, dispute Beano's strategy and try to go his own way?

Beano shook his head. He had to stop counting things that could go wrong, football strategies that might be misdirected. He had to believe in his players—and in himself.

Mrs. Hatton walked through the kitchen. She glanced at the untouched sandwich. "You'd better eat, even if you're not hungry," she said. "It's going to be a long evening."

Beano remembered that he was hungry. "Yeah, okay," he said, picking up the sandwich and taking a bite.

"Your father should be home about five o'clock or a little after. What time do you need to go back to the school?"

"Around six. I ought to be there, I guess, when the Carterville team arrives, to make sure they go to the right dressing room and all that."

After glancing at the kitchen clock to check the time, Beano's mother left, to be replaced by Jeremy.

Jeremy looked at the sandwich and said, "All I got was a cookie. Mom said any more would spoil my supper."

"This is my supper," Beano said.

Jeremy slid into a chair opposite his brother and asked, "What are you going to wear?"

"Wear? When?"

"For the game. Coach Pritchard always wore a suit. Are you going to wear a suit at the game now that you're the coach?"

Beano grimaced. "No, I'm not going to wear a suit."

"That coach on television last Saturday—the Purdue coach, you know—he was wearing a warmup suit with football shoes and a cap. Remember?"

"You sure notice a lot about what football coaches wear."

"Well, what are you going to wear?"

"I'm going to wear what I've got on right now, with maybe a sweater under the jacket. There, does that satisfy you?"

Jeremy looked disappointed.

Beano was in his room, seated at his desk, reviewing his game plan once again, when his father arrived. Beano did not hear the car pulling into the driveway nor his father coming into the house.

"Hey, coach!" his father's voice rang out.

Beano laid aside the clipboard and went downstairs. They hugged, and then Beano, in what had become a family custom, carried his father's bag up to his parents' bedroom while his father took off his overcoat and hung it up in the entryway closet.

On his way back down, Beano stopped off in his room and picked up his clipboard. He wanted it on top of his jacket on the chair downstairs, so it could not possibly be left behind.

Then he joined his parents and Jeremy at the kitchen table.

"All set?" his father asked.

"Beano's going to wear his regular clothes, instead of a suit and tie or something," Jeremy announced.

Beano gave Jeremy a sharp glance, shook his head, and turned back to his father. "I think everything's set," Beano said. Then he managed a small smile and added, "But I won't know for sure until the game is over."

"You've always been good at figuring things out—and good at getting things done—and I'm sure everything is in place and ready to go. It'll work like a charm. You wait and see."

Beano watched his father. He wondered whether his father knew that Marty had quit the team and then returned. Probably so, Beano decided. His father always stopped by the office on the way home when returning from a trip. For sure, everyone in Barton was still talking about Marty leaving and coming back. Somebody in the office would have mentioned it. But it was, Beano knew, so like his father to leave the subject of Marty unmentioned in these minutes leading up to the game.

"Irrelevant now," he probably would say if some-body—and Beano glanced at Jeremy—mentioned the episode.

"But you know what they say," Beano said, "the football can take some funny bounces."

. "If that happens, you can't help it. But I'm sure that all the players will be giving everything they've got to win this one."

Did his father put emphasis on the word "all," meaning Marty Tucker? Beano thought so.

"It's about time for me to go," Beano said.

Mr. Hatton drove Beano to the school, and they arrived just as two green-and-white buses bearing the Carterville team pulled onto the parking lot next to the building.

The lights were on above the bleachers on either side of the playing field. The dazzling arc lights that illuminated the field during the game would not be turned on until the last minute because of the great expense involved. But in the glow from the bleacher lights, an occasional figure was visible moving around. The ticket sellers, ticket takers, and ushers were getting themselves organized for their game-night duties. Lights from inside the school building showed through the windows around the area of the dressing rooms.

Otherwise the whole area was empty and dark.

Beano leaped out of his father's car, heard him call out "Good luck," replied, "Thanks," and ran toward the first of the two Carterville High buses.

In the glare of the headlights, Beano waved the bus to a halt. Then he walked around to the door, which swung open as he got there.

A burly man with short-cut reddish hair, about the age of Beano's father, stepped down.

"Coach Prescott?"

The man answered, "Yes, that's right," eyeing Beano with open curiosity.

"I'm Beano Hatton." Beano extended his right hand. "I'm pleased to meet you."

Coach Prescott looked at Beano's hand for a moment, then took it, and they shook. "*Hubert* Hatton?"

"Everybody calls me Beano."

Coach Prescott studied Beano for a moment with undisguised amazement. Then he gave a little smile and said, "Beano, then."

"Your drivers can pull around behind the school building. That way," Beano said, waving an arm, "and park near the door with the light above it. I'll meet you inside and show you to your dressing room."

"All right. Thanks."

Beano turned and walked toward the school building.

Behind him, he heard through an open window of the bus someone saying, "Is he the one who's their coach?"

By then Beano was too far away to hear the reply.

Beano sat on the training table in the dressing room while the players suited up for the game. The room was deathly quiet. Beano did not know whether that was good or bad. With Coach Pritchard on the scene, the pregame dressing room was always a mix of somber intensity and nervous joking and laughing. But Coach Pritchard was not on the scene tonight.

Beano waited as the players finished dressing and one by one turned toward him.

Marty was seated on a bench, his elbows on his knees, hands clasped, staring at the floor.

From outside, a rhythmic roar announced that the pep band was starting up and the cheerleaders were going to work. That meant that most of the fans were in their seats. It was almost time to take the field.

The last player to pull his jersey over his head and down over his shoulder pads—Bud

Holland—turned and looked toward Beano.

Beano slid off the training table and stood next to it. Marty looked up. Beano scanned the faces around the room. He took a breath.

"I've never delivered a pep talk, and I'm not going to try it tonight," he said. He half expected someone—probably Edwin Deere—to pipe up with something like "Thank heaven!" But nobody said anything. The room remained quiet. "But I am going to remind you of some of the things we've all heard Coach Pritchard say in the past."

Beano felt foolish, the student manager lecturing the football players. But then he told himself that he wasn't the student manager. He was the acting coach. The student manager was Denny Overman, standing over there by Todd Bowman and giving him a quick nod of encouragement.

Beano plunged ahead. "Football is really a very simple game. You've all heard Coach Pritchard say that. Football is just running and tackling and blocking and passing and catching. That's all. Very simple. What really counts is how well you do those things. That's what Coach Pritchard always said. Well, what I'm going to say is that Coach Pritchard taught you how to do those things, and if you do them well in the game tonight, we'll come out winners."

Beano looked around at the serious faces. Okay so far. At least nobody was laughing or hooting. Marty Tucker, expressionless, was watching Beano closely. Even Edwin Deere wore a sober expression.

"When two teams are about equal—and we are about even with the Bobcats—the team that wants to win the most is the team that will win. You've heard Coach Pritchard say that. I know that we are the ones who want to win the most. We've got a very big reason to want to bring home the victory."

Beano paused for a deep breath.

"A third and final point," he said. "We've all heard Coach Pritchard say that more football games are lost than won. We know what he meant—mistakes lose games. A team that might have won becomes a loser instead of a winner because of mistakes. And a team that by all rights should have lost becomes a winner because of the opponent's mistakes. So let's make no mistakes tonight."

Beano stopped. He was finished. He wished that someone would cheer or shout or just say something. But nobody did.

He walked to the door, opened it, and stood holding it. "Okay," he said. "Let's go."

Beano watched the players filing past him—Todd, Bud, Art, Marty, all of them—and wondered what was going through their minds.

Determination? Let's win this one for Coach Pritchard?

Or portents of doom? We're playing this game without our coach.

When the last of the players had gone by and Beano closed the door and followed them down the corridor, he concluded that he did not have the faintest idea what the Barton High Tigers were thinking, or what was going to happen on the field.

Chapter 14

When Beano came out of the school building, the first of the players ahead of him was already jogging through the opening in the chain-link fence and onto the field.

A loud roar went up from the bleachers on both sides of the field, and the pep band blared. The arc lights, now on, bathed the playing field in a shimmering glow.

The Barton High Tigers, in their gold uniforms with black trim, moved into lines in the end zone for their warm-up bends and stretches.

Beano, his clipboard under his arm, broke into a trot to the gate, then slowed to a walk and went through, taking up a position at the end-zone sideline.

At the other end of the field, the Carterville Bobcats, in their white uniforms with green trim, were already in place, moving through their warm-up calisthenics.

Maybe, Beano thought, the Carterville coach had not needed to take the time for a pre-game talk in the dressing room.

Beano heard shouts of his name—"Bean-oh! Bean-oh!"—and turned and glanced at the bleachers. The packed crowd in the bleachers behind the Tigers' bench was dotted with black and gold. A lot of people wore clothing in the Barton High colors—a jacket, or just a cap, in black and gold. Some of the people waved pom-poms. From the look of it, even the aisles and steps were filled with people. The bleachers across the field were the same, except for a large square of people at the forty-yard line wearing green and white. A lot of Carterville fans had made the short drive for the game. The rivalry always drew a good crowd, but this time there was the added attraction for both sides of watching Beano Hatton, student manager, coach the home team.

Beano looked back at the bleachers behind the Tigers' bench. His father and mother and Jeremy were up there somewhere, he knew. He turned back to the Barton High players lined up in the end zone, now bending and stretching under Marty's leadership.

Then Beano heard his name again, not a shout from the bleachers but a call from behind him.

He turned and saw Denny coming toward him.

"Bert says Mr. Abernathy needs the starting lineup for the loudspeaker announcement," Denny said.

Beano looked beyond Denny and saw Bert Moore, a boy about the size of Beano, waiting on the cinder track. Bert always sat next to Mr. Abernathy in the press box, helping spot players' numbers for Mr. Abernathy's loudspeaker announcements of ball carriers and tacklers after each play. Beano glanced at the jammed bleachers and thought that Bert must have had a tough time making his way down through the crowd from the press box, and faced a tough climb back.

"He says that Coach Pritchard always gave it to you, and you delivered it," Denny said.

Beano had forgotten. He wondered what other details he might have forgotten—details that would rise up on the playing field during the game and cost the Tigers points. Well, at least this oversight cost no points.

"Tell him it's the same as last week," Beano said. "No changes." Then he added, "And ask Bert to tell Mr. Abernathy that I'm sorry for the trouble, but I just forgot."

Denny nodded and turned and ran to the cinder track to give Bert the word.

Beano looked up at the press box and gave a little wave to Mr. Abernathy, who was leaning forward watching them.

Marty was winding down the warm-up calisthenics and the players moved into signal drills.

Beano walked up the sideline toward the bench, watching Marty begin taking snaps from the center and running or handing off.

Marty seemed to have accepted all of Beano's game plan. He had not objected to a single point. He did not speak a word of protest or ask a single question. While Dave had kept saying, "Yeah" and "Gee, sure" and "Okay, right," Marty gave a nod, nothing more, to each point.

Beano had to concede that Marty had taken the points only without speaking any objections. He had not really acknowledged that he accepted them.

Beano gave a little shrug as he reached midfield along the sideline. He knew what he would do—would have to do—if Marty failed to follow his directions. If Marty tried to go his own way, Beano would replace him with Dave immediately.

Marty Tucker and Larry Slider, the Tigers' co-captains, walked to the center of the field to meet the Carterville co-captains for the toss of the coin.

The players shook hands and the referee flipped the coin into the air and let it fall to the ground. Everyone bent over to look at it.

Larry shot a fist in the air, and Beano knew the Tigers had won the toss. So did the fans in the bleachers. They sent up a cheer.

Beano drew a deep breath and thought, Well, at least we won something that was worth a cheer.

Marty, as instructed by Beano, told the referee that the Tigers wanted to receive the opening kick-off. That would have been Marty's choice anyway, Beano knew.

The Bobcats' co-captains chose to defend the goal to Beano's right, which did not matter at all on this cold but windless evening.

The referee signaled the results of the coin toss, and Marty and Larry turned and ran back to the bench. Immediately, they and Beano were sur-rounded by a mob of cheering players slapping each other on the shoulder pads.

Disappearing in the midst of players a head taller than he, Beano shouted, "Let's go! Let's go!"

The players were lined up.

Todd Bowman was back deep, on the fifteen-yard line, awaiting the kickoff. He stood with his left foot slightly forward, his arms dangling loosely at his sides. In front of him, his blockers were arrayed in position.

Beyond the Barton High blockers, the Carterville kicker was out in front of the row of his teammates, placing the ball for the kick.

Beano, his jacket collar now turned up against the cold of the night, stood at the sideline with his clipboard in his hand and stared at the scene. It seemed eerie, the shadowless field under the arc lights, the sudden quiet of the people in the bleachers, all of them on their feet.

Marty, ready to take the field after the kickoff, stood on the sidelines a half-dozen yards to Beano's left. He was holding his helmet in his right hand, staring into space.

All along the sidelines the Barton High players stood, almost somberly at this moment, and waited.

The Carterville kicker backed off from the tilted football, then stopped and waited for the referee's signal. He got it and moved forward, swinging his right foot into the ball.

On both sides of the kicker the rows of Carterville tacklers surged forward.

In front of them the Barton High blockers began moving into position.

The kick was straight and high but short.

Todd, his head tilted back, watching, moved forward to bring himself under the falling ball.

At the sideline, Beano unconsciously lifted the clipboard up under his arm and wiped his perspiring hands on his jacket. He wondered, How does a coach make sure the receiver doesn't fumble the opening kickoff?

Todd took another couple of steps forward and caught the ball. He tucked it away as he crossed the twenty-yard line and ran straight ahead, toward a crowd of gold-jerseyed Tigers trying to blast open a path for him.

Beano felt the need for a deep breath, and he took it. Todd had not fumbled the opening kickoff. He was running with the ball toward his blockers.

Todd crossed the twenty-five-yard line, then the thirty, and plunged on toward his blockers at midfield.

Beano realized that his left fist was tightly clenched and his right hand held the clipboard in a death grip. Take it easy, he thought. This is only the first play.

A white-clad Carterville tackler crashed

through and slammed Todd to the ground on the thirty-six-yard line.

Marty was pulling on his helmet and dashing onto the field almost before Todd hit the ground.

Todd returned to the sideline to sit out one play and catch his breath. Beano walked across and clapped him on the shoulder pads. "Good running," he said.

But Beano's mind wasn't on Todd. He turned immediately to the playing field. Marty had his instructions for the first series of downs. They were, Beano knew, probably the same instructions that Coach Pritchard would have delivered. He had not watched Coach Pritchard for three years without learning them. Presumably Marty knew too that Beano's instructions followed Coach Pritchard's ideas. But was he going to follow them this time?

Marty handed off to the fullback, Thurman Lowry, plunging off right tackle. Thurman gained four yards to the forty-yard line.

Todd raced back onto the field, and Marty promptly pitched out to him running around left end. Todd cut back in and wriggled his way to the forty-six-yard line, for a six-yard gain and a first down.

Beano decided it was safe to resume breathing

normally. Nothing terrible had happened. Todd hadn't fumbled the kickoff. Marty was calling the prescribed plays. As a matter of fact, good things were happening. The Tigers had run two plays for gains and a first down. Beano heard the cheers of the crowd in the bleachers.

Marty connected on a short pass to Art Fleming, but the gain was only three yards. Then Marty missed on a throw to Joe Burgess.

Third down and seven to go for a first down.

It was a passing situation, and Marty knew it as well as Beano. Beano was confident that Marty would throw, because he loved being the passing quarterback. The only problem, Beano reflected, was that the Carterville Bobcats knew as well as Marty and Beano that the situation called for a pass. And the Carterville coach, surely having done his homework, would know that Marty liked to pass. If Beano could have caught Marty's eye, he would have signaled a draw play up the middle, hoping that the unexpected would catch the Bobcats off their guard and charging in to stop a pass. But Marty wasn't looking to the sidelines for advice.

Marty took the snap and rolled out to his right. The Carterville linebackers hit the line with a blitz. Art Fleming dashed straight forward, then veered toward the sideline, looking back for the ball. Marty stopped, cocked his arm, and threw, barely getting the ball away before a charging tackler knocked him to the ground.

The hurried pass was falling short. Art slammed on the brakes, turned, and raced back toward the ball.

A Carterville defender beat Art to the ball, got a hand on it, juggled the ball a moment, then lost it.

Beano, no longer breathing normally, felt his heart leap into his throat. He let out a long breath when the ball finally hit the ground—an incompletion instead of an interception.

Fourth down and seven—an obvious punting situation.

Beano turned back to Marty, now getting back to his feet. But Marty did not return Beano's glance. He turned his back to the Barton High sideline and headed for the huddle.

Beano called out to his departing back: "Marty!"

Marty did not turn. Clearly the quarterback had no intention of taking signals from Acting Coach Beano Hatton, former student manager.

"Marty!" Beano called again.

Marty was at the huddle.

Todd and Thurman both turned at Beano's

shout. If they had heard, so had Marty. But he did not turn.

Beano saw Todd say something to Marty, and after a moment, Marty turned and looked at Beano.

Beano went through the motion of dusting off his hands—the only signal he had added to Coach Pritchard's repertoire: the signal for a fake punt and run if the Bobcats packed the line of scrimmage with ten players.

Marty's expression showed that he knew what was coming. He scowled at Beano.

Beano said to himself, barely aloud, "I'm trying to make a hero out of you, you stupid jerk." Marty surely could not object to the play. But he could object to Beano Hatton being the one who devised it, and now the one who was calling for it.

Beano returned Marty's glare and then, without thinking, lifted his hand and made the motion of cutting his throat.

Marty got the meaning. If he didn't follow directions, he was coming out of the game. His mouth opened slightly, then closed.

Marty leaned into the huddle, said something, and the Tigers broke the huddle and lined up in punt formation with Marty back deep, awaiting the snap from center.

The Bobcats shifted into a ten-man line, hoping to crash through and block the kick or, at the least, force Marty into a hurried and poor kick. They had one player back deep to field the punt if the charge failed.

Marty extended his hands and barked the signals: "Hup! Hup! Hup!"

The snap from center led Marty slightly to the left, as intended. The hope was that from the tangle of bodies at the line of scrimmage, the snap would simply look like a bad one, not a lead to give Marty a half-step advantage.

Marty took in the ball and shifted into high gear, heading around left end.

Todd ran inside of Marty with the assignment of taking out the first Carterville tackler to approach and challenge Marty. Todd did his job, falling in front of the first Bobcat player to make it through.

Marty ran on in a wide sweep, making his cut and heading downfield.

Art Fleming, from his tight-end position, raced straight ahead downfield. His assignment was to take out the Bobcats' punt returner, the last player with a shot at tackling Marty.

A roar rolled down from the bleachers as the Barton High fans leaped to their feet as one.

Marty crossed the fifty-yard line, the forty-five, the forty.

Behind him no one was within fifteen yards of him.

Ahead of him the punt returner was moving across and forward, watching Marty.

Then Art appeared, running with Marty, keeping himself between Marty and the punt returner.

The punt returner hesitated in the face of the threat from Art, and Marty ran past him and into the end zone.

Chapter 15

Beano, clipboard in hand, ran down the sideline past the row of screaming, shouting Barton High Tigers while Marty circled in the end zone and then ran into a big hug from Art.

The roaring cheer of the crowd in the bleachers was deafening, and to Beano the arc lights bathing the field seemed to glow even more brightly.

As he ran, Beano glanced up at the scoreboard behind the end zone. The lights blinked: Tigers 6, Visitors 0.

He met Marty coming off the field at the twenty-yard line. "Beautiful! Beautiful running!" Beano shouted at him above the din of the crowd.

Marty draped an arm around Beano's thin shoulder, gave a brief squeeze, and then jogged on toward his cheering teammates.

Beano turned to Art and called out, "Great play! Perfect!"

Art was grinning as he jogged past.

Beano felt his heart pounding in his chest. He knew that if his smile widened another fraction of an inch, his face probably would split in two. He watched Marty wade into the crowd of excited teammates shouting their congratulations.

What a difference one play could make—maybe.

Beano gave a little shrug at the thought. The Tigers had scored, and he was willing to settle for that, for now.

He began walking back toward his position at the midfield sideline while the kicking team lined up for the extra point.

Randy Wolfe kicked good out of Marty's hold, and the scoreboard changed to 7-0.

The Bobcats took the kickoff and began a methodical march down the field.

In action the Carterville offense fitted perfectly the descriptions the two coaches had given Beano on the telephone. The Bobcats hit the line more often than not—one side, then the other, then the middle—probing and testing the strengths and weaknesses of the Barton High defense. They broke up their hammering into the line with an occasional end run. All of it was very simple. The handoffs were straight, without even a hint of a fake. Nothing tricky at all. Not even a pass. Just a game of power, settling for short gains.

To Beano, kneeling at the sideline, the scene was scary. As they ground away, the Bobcats looked as unstoppable as a steamroller.

True, there was no sign of anything explosive in their attack. They had no speedster capable of breaking into the open and outrunning everyone to the goal from anywhere on the field on any given play. And obviously they did not want to pass. They were not going to strike quickly through the air for a touchdown. No, there was no fear that in the blink of an eye they were going to even the score with one spectacular play.

But they had big linemen and strong backs, and they took no chances—and the combination was eating up the yards and gaining one first down after another.

They rolled across the fifty-yard line and moved on. They were getting three yards off tackle, five yards up the middle, four yards in the left side of the line. On and on.

With a first down on the Barton High thirty-four-yard line, the Bobcats looked sure to rumble, slowly but surely, all the way to the goal.

In addition to gobbling up yardage, they were

running out the clock, maintaining control of the ball, and leaving the Tigers' offense helplessly waiting on the sidelines.

Through it all Beano knelt, unmoving, at the sideline and watched.

As the teams lined up yet one more time—the Carterville offense versus the Barton defense—the buzzer sounded, ending the first quarter.

The noise startled Beano and he stood up. The game was one-fourth over. Already?

Mr. Abernathy's familiar voice came over the loudspeaker, announcing that Coach Pritchard was doing well and was listening to the radio broadcast of the game in his hospital bed.

The fans in the bleachers applauded, and several sent up cheers.

Beano, moving down the sideline as the teams changed ends of the field, glanced up at the press box and wondered if Zip Logan had mentioned the problem with Marty on the air. Probably not, he decided. Probably Principal Tyler had cautioned him that Coach Pritchard would be listening to the broadcast of the game, and that the coach did not—and should not—know about Marty quitting the team for a day.

As the applause and cheers for the good news about Coach Pritchard faded, Beano was aware of a silence in the bleachers and among the players lining the sidelines. The Barton High fans and players alike recognized the threat of the plodding, battering Carterville offense. Nobody in black and gold felt like cheering at the turn the game was taking.

Again the teams lined up. The Carterville center snapped the ball. The quarterback took it, turned, stepped back, and extended the ball to the fullback charging over guard.

More of the same.

The fullback broke through and found himself face to face with Larry Slider. It was the setting for a classic collision, the powerful fullback plunging forward with full momentum, the strong linebacker leaning forward and driving off his right foot.

Beano heard the sound—*whomp!*—of the collision.

Beano rose from his kneeling position at the sideline for a better look. He saw the fullback lose his footing as Larry, the stronger of the two, lifted him and threw him back.

Then Beano saw the ball in the air, floating, just hanging there. A gold-jerseyed Barton High player moved between Beano and the ball, blocking his view. Then both player and ball disappeared behind the tangle of players at the line of scrimmage.

Beano unconsciously took a step forward, his right hand clutching his clipboard, his left knotted into a tight fist.

Then he saw, almost simultaneously, the referee gesturing Barton High's possession of the ball and Bud Holland lifting a triumphant fist in the air, adding his own signal that one of his teammates had recovered the loose ball.

Beano stepped back and let out a breath.

Barton High's ball on the Tiger thirty-one-yard line.

Pete Claiborne, the Tigers' right tackle, danced a brief jig of delight, accepted the congratulations of his teammates on the field, and ran to the sideline with both hands in the air.

Beano looked for Marty, found him, and called out—"Marty!"

Marty, pulling on his helmet, was already two steps onto the playing field.

"Marty!"

Marty stopped and turned back toward Beano. His expression was half questioning, half irritation. "What?" he said.

"The first series," Beano said. "Right?"

Marty gave a little nod that Beano thought looked a bit grudging, acknowledging that the same plays they had used in their first possession were the best plays for now, starting this far back in their own territory.

Thurman Lowry got six yards off right tackle and Todd Bowman gained five around left end, giving the Tigers a first down on their forty-two-yard line.

Beano stood at the sideline and watched as the Tigers huddled. Marty made a point of not glancing at Beano to see if there were any signals. Beano remained silent and unmoving. He knew what Marty wanted to do next—pass. Marty always wanted to pass. And in this situation, that was all right with Beano. For now, he tried to stifle his rising anger at Marty for so pointedly ignoring him.

Marty hit Art Fleming twice, first on a button hook at the sideline for six yards and then over the middle for five yards and another first down. The Tigers, on the Bobcats' forty-eight-yard line, were moving.

Marty ran an option to the right for three yards, then passed to Todd in the left flat for five yards.

Third down and two to go for a first down on the Carterville forty-yard line.

The situation was tailor-made for one of two plays, either a quarterback sneak, with Marty strong enough to bull his way forward for two yards, or Thurman Lowry plunging off tackle. Thurman could always gain two yards, and Beano was sure that Thurman would have been Coach Pritchard's choice.

Beano was also sure that Marty knew he had a choice of two plays.

Marty, leaning into the huddle, again avoided glancing in Beano's direction.

Beano had a funny feeling—a small echo of a doubt in his mind—and started to shout. But then he didn't. Marty surely knew the right play. He'd taken signals from Coach Pritchard for three years.

The Tigers broke the huddle and lined up.

Beano raised an eyebrow when he saw Art Fleming take up a position a couple of yards wider than needed for a run into the line. For an instant Beano couldn't believe his eyes. When Art, lining up, turned to Beano with a questioning expression, Beano felt his face suddenly flush red. He stepped forward to call for a time-out.

But the ball had been snapped.

Marty faked a handoff to Thurman plunging into the line, then rolled back, scanning the field for a receiver.

Art was running straight ahead down the right sideline.

Todd was angling out into the left flat.

Both were open.

But it didn't matter. The Carterville linemen, charging hard to gain dominance of the line of scrimmage, were breaking through while Marty weighed his decision and then cocked his arm for a long throw. They were zeroing in on him before he could throw. Marty brought down the ball and tucked it away. He managed to duck the first lineman coming at him. He turned and scrambled forward, the only hope left of making the needed two yards for a first down.

The second Carterville lineman coming in got him, dumping Marty on the forty-three-yard line, a loss of three yards.

Now it was fourth down and five yards to go.

For sure Marty did not look at Beano now—not when he was getting up after the tackle, not when he leaned into the huddle, and not when he broke the huddle and lined up in punt formation.

But Beano looked at Marty. He never took his

eyes off him, from the tackle to the punting position. Beano fought to control the rage that was seething within him. It seemed, he thought, that Marty called the wrong play just to show himself and Beano—and the whole world—who was in charge. Marty Tucker was not taking directions from Beano Hatton. But maybe that wasn't it. Maybe Marty just made a serious judgment error. Either way, the mistake should not have been made. Beano clenched his teeth and decided that he shouldn't say to Marty what he really wanted to say. The word "stupid" kept dancing through his mind. Then Beano decided what he should say, and the word "stupid" was not included.

Marty punted, and the Carterville receiver called for a fair catch, taking in the ball on the twenty-four-yard line.

Beano noticed that the Bobcats did not line up ten players on the line of scrimmage for a punt this time.

Marty came off the field, removing his helmet as he walked, and took up a position at the sideline about ten yards to Beano's left.

Beano immediately turned and walked up to him.

Marty seemed in deep concentration watching the Bobcats run their first play, a plunge into the middle of the line, and gave no indication he was aware of Beano's arrival at his side.

The players who were scattered along the sidelines noticed though, and more of them were watching the quarterback and the acting coach than were looking at the play on the field.

Beano gave it a couple of seconds and then stepped around in front of Marty and looked up into his face.

Before Beano could speak, Marty said, "I figured they'd be looking for Thurman in the line, and that a pass would surprise them—had touchdown written all over it." He forced a little smile and added, "Almost worked, too."

Beano would have liked to point out that "almost" never won a football game. But he decided to say what he had come to say and not respond to Marty's feeble explanation. "I have two things to say to you," he said softly.

Marty looked down at Beano with a bland expression and said nothing.

"One, you are to look at me before every play and follow any instruction I give."

Marty's face broke into a patronizing grin. "And?" he said.

"Two, if you don't, we'll change quarterbacks."

The smile left Marty's face.

Beano turned and walked along the sideline back to his post at midfield.

Chapter 16

The Carterville Bobcats, sticking to their running game, rolled upfield to the fifty-yard line. They were hitting the middle, going off tackle, circling the ends. Noticeably, they were avoiding the left side of their line, where Larry Slider's giant form awaited the ball carrier. They were eating up yardage and eating up minutes with their grinding ground game, leaving the Barton High offensive unit watching from the sidelines.

Then, as if he'd had enough, Larry Slider suddenly was everywhere on the field at the same time. If a Carterville runner had the ball, Larry was there to meet him. The Carterville offense had been trying to avoid his crushing tackles. But now it was impossible, because wherever the ball went, Larry went.

With three consecutive tackles—a blitz that caught the halfback for a loss, a diving tackle that knocked down the sturdy fullback, and a chase to the sidelines that doomed an end run—Larry left the Bobcats facing fourth down and four yards to go on the Barton High forty-three-yard line.

As the teams lined up in punt formation, Beano looked around for Marty. He found him and walked over to him.

"Keep it on the ground until we're out of the hole, and then throw," he said. "But keep the throws short."

Beano knew that his advice was obvious. Passing was a dangerous tactic deep in the Tigers' own territory. Marty knew that as well as Beano. But Beano wanted his statement on record with the quarterback. He did not want a repeat of Marty's creative thinking in play selection. Beano knew that when the time came to pass, he could count on accuracy from Marty with the short, quick passes. But he was erratic with his long throws—a shortcoming Marty did not readily acknowledge— and Beano did not want him uncorking a long pass off the mark for an interception. He wanted that statement—short passes only—on the record with Marty too.

Marty looked at Beano as if he had not spoken, and said nothing in response.

Maybe, Beano thought, Marty was waiting to

be reminded that he must look at him before every play. But Beano did no reminding. It was up to Marty to remember. Beano silently returned Marty's gaze.

Finally Marty gave a little nod.

Beano nodded in return, then turned and walked away from Marty to watch the punt.

On the field, Todd was circling under a high punt. The Carterville tacklers were bearing down on him.

Beano instinctively said to himself, "Fair catch."

Too bad, but without a runback the Tigers were going to have to start their drive deep, deep in their own territory.

But Todd did not raise his hand to stop the tacklers and allow himself to bring in the ball safely. Todd was going to try to catch the ball in the shadow of thundering tacklers and make a run for it.

Todd caught the ball on the fifteen-yard line and turned quickly, avoiding the rush of the first tackler in on him. Holding the ball dangerously away from his body, he swerved out of the grasp of a second tackler and raced upfield, angling toward the sideline. A Carterville tackler finally knocked him out of bounds at the thirty-one-yard line.

Marty led the offensive unit onto the field to take up the attack.

Todd jogged to the sideline to take a breather for one play, and Beano met him.

"Nice running," Beano said.

Todd puffed, "Thanks."

"But you realize, of course, that Coach Pritchard probably would have had you tied to the mast and flogged for not signaling a fair catch."

"Yeah." Todd grinned at Beano. "But I didn't want to leave us stuck on the fifteen-yard line."

As they talked, Beano kept his eyes on Marty. Going into the huddle, Marty glanced at Beano. Beano responded with a curt nod.

Then Beano turned to Todd. "Better to be stuck on the fifteen-yard line with the ball than fumbling over to Carterville on the fifteen-yard line."

"Okay, okay, you're right."

Thurman Lowry hit the middle of the line, driving his way forward for a four-yard gain.

"But it was a nice run," Beano told Todd with a laugh. Then he turned and walked back up the sideline to the fifty-yard line, and Todd raced back into the game.

With a couple of line plunges, an end run, and

two short passes—one to Art Fleming and one to Joe Burgess—Marty led the Tigers to two first downs and across the fifty-yard line.

Before each play, Marty glanced at Beano at the sideline, and Beano nodded in return.

Marty was calling the plays, which surely pleased Marty. And Marty was calling the right plays, which pleased Beano.

Maybe, Beano thought with a sigh, we'll all survive this football game. He turned and looked at the bleachers, wondering again where his parents and Jeremy were seated. Then he glanced up at the press box. He could see Zip Logan speaking into his microphone. Beano knew that at the hospital Coach Pritchard was listening to what Zip Logan was saying.

Beano turned his attention back to the field.

The last second of the first half ticked away with the score unchanged: Barton 7, Carterville 0.

Beano, lost in the crowd of players jogging off the field toward the dressing room, turned over in his mind the problems he saw facing the Tigers in the second half.

The battering Carterville ground game was taking its toll on the Barton High defensive unit. Already there were signs of weariness. It was going to get worse in the second half unless the Tigers could stop the relentless running attack, take the ball away from Carterville, and give the Barton High defenders some resting time on the sidelines. So far the Tigers' defense had kept Carterville from scoring. But a tiring defense was not going to be able to hold off the Bobcats forever. Beano resolved that he needed to substitute more freely.

And he resolved to start the second half with the three-linebacker configuration—surely something was needed to blunt the Bobcats' running attack. True, the three-linebacker configuration was new to the Tigers, but, Beano thought with satisfaction, it would be new to Carterville, too.

Still, Beano could not escape the conclusion that the Carterville Bobcats were sure to score. The steam-roller ground game was bound to power its way into the end zone at least once.

And that led to a second problem Beano saw facing the Tigers in the second half.

The Tigers had scored only once—and that on the fake punt. They had not succeeded in driving down the field and punching across the goal. For sure, the Tigers were going to have to score again— at least once, maybe more—in order to win the game.

But how?

The players and Beano reached the school building and poured through the door, down the corridor, and into the dressing room.

A frowning Beano headed for the training table and laid his clipboard on it. He let the players have a moment to themselves while he thumbed through the sheets of paper on the clipboard. Something on those pages had to spark an idea.

Behind him the players were quiet. Beano heard an occasional softly spoken word. He heard somebody loudly swishing out his mouth with water. He heard the shuffle of players moving about, slowly, leisurely, savoring the relief from speed and collision.

Beano finally smoothed down the sheets of paper on the clipboard. Nothing spectacular had been discovered in his scribblings. There was no secret formula for victory. Just plain football, well played. He took a breath and turned to face the players.

The room was silent, and everyone was looking at him.

In the distance the Barton High band was blaring. Maybe the band was standing in the middle of the field. Beano didn't know. He had not seen the band perform at halftime in his three years as student manager. He was always in the dressing room at halftime.

"We've got to stop the Carterville ground attack, and give our defense some time to rest, and give our offense more time on the field," he said. "And we've got to score."

Again silence.

"We'll start the second half with three linebackers, like we worked it in the scrimmage on Wednesday—Larry in the middle, Chickie on the left as usual, and Clark Gray on the right. We'll go down to two, instead of three, defensive backs—Barney Meddaugh and Billy Hale."

Beano paused. He wasn't sure what to expect. As acting coach, the decision was his. The responsibility, if something went wrong, was his too. Well, he had made the decision. Now to see if anyone objected.

"Are you sure—" It was Marty Tucker looking up from his seat on a bench.

Beano interrupted him. "Marty, we'll get to the offense in just a minute."

Several players exchanged glances. Nobody ever told Marty Tucker that something was none of his business. But that was what Beano had just done, with one simple sentence.

Marty looked surprised, and then puzzled. Then he recovered. "Coach Pritchard always said the smart thing to do was to stick to what you know," he said.

Beano let the comment go unanswered for a moment. He looked around. Larry Slider appeared pleased at the prospect of playing middle linebacker. Instead of guarding one side of the line, he was going to be in a better position to chase off after the ball carrier anywhere on the field. Clark Gray sat quite still, waiting silently for any argument about the decision to send him from the bench into the game.

Larry broke the silence, speaking to Marty instead of Beano. "Beano's right," he said. "Those guys haven't thrown a single pass. All they do is run. We need to set ourselves up to stop the run. We're wasting a man with three defensive backs."

"Clark and I can watch the flanks," Chickie said.

Beano moved to stop the talk. Next thing he knew, somebody would be proposing a vote on the question. He remembered what he had heard Coach Pritchard say once: "A football team is not a democracy. We don't decide anything by majority rule. I am the coach, and I decide."

So Beano took a breath, waved a hand, and said, "Hold it a minute."

The room fell silent.

"We'll do it—at least give it a try with three linebackers and two defensive backs," Beano said. "If it works, great. If we have trouble, we can go back to our usual formation."

He glanced at Chickie and Clark and said, "This may drive 'em, or tempt 'em, to try some passes. You'll have to be careful."

They nodded back at him.

"Okay," Beano said. "Now the offense."

Marty straightened up on the bench, looking to be ready for anything.

But Marty wasn't ready for what Beano said.

"I've got one idea," Beano said. "It came out of the practice on Thursday when Dave was working at quarterback with the first team."

Marty frowned. He did not enjoy a reference to the Thursday practice, when he had quit the team and someone else was playing quarterback.

"Dave can throw long," Beano said. "We saw it in practice on Thursday." Beano looked over at Dave. "I'm going to send you in, Dave, for spot duty when we can afford to spend a play on a long pass."

Dave smiled and bobbed his head in agreement.

Marty said, "Now, wait a minute—"

Beano continued without acknowledging Marty's protest. "The Bobcats are big and strong, but they're not fast. Art and Joe, you can outrun 'em, right?"

Art and Joe gave small nods.

"There's another thing," Beano said. "We haven't thrown long more than a half-dozen times all season." He decided not to mention that one attempt was Marty's unsuccessful effort despite Beano's wishes in the first half. "The Carterville coach, and his players, surely know that we don't throw long. So we'll have the surprise element on our side."

As Beano spoke, Todd, seated next to Marty on the bench, leaned in and said something to him. Marty gave Todd a sharp glance but said nothing.

Beano stood at the sideline holding the clipboard in his right hand. He was not going to need it and its stack of pages in the second half. He had made his decisions, and either they would work— or not. But he still held the clipboard in his hand. It felt good.

On the field, Randy Wolfe was teeing up the football for the Tigers' kickoff to the Bobcats to begin the second half. In the bleachers on both sides of the field, the fans were on their feet.

Beano turned and looked up at the press box at the top of the bleachers. He saw Zip Logan chattering into his microphone. Zip's jaw was going to drop when the Tigers lined up on defense with three linebackers and two defensive backs. And when Zip recovered from the shock and made the announcement into his microphone, Coach Pritchard was probably going to fall off his bed at the hospital. And he will fall off the bed again, Beano figured, when he hears that Beano has sent Dave Harris into the game at quarterback.

Beano turned back toward the field, leaving such thoughts behind, and watched.

Randy backed away from the ball and awaited the referee's signal.

Chapter 17

The kick was high and short. The Carterville receiver raced forward and took in the ball on the twenty-one-yard line, then went down under three Barton High tacklers.

The Bobcats huddled, then broke and lined up—and saw for the first time what they were facing.

The combination of a six-man line and three linebackers must have looked like a thick stone wall to a quarterback planning to hand off for a line plunge.

Beyond the linebackers, Barney Meddaugh and Billy Hale divided the space where a pass receiver might take in the ball.

To Beano, accustomed to watching Coach Pritchard's three-man secondary, the space being patroled by only Barney and Billy now seemed recklessly wide open. Did it appear wide open—

tantalizingly so—to the Carterville quarterback?

Beano looked at the Carterville quarterback. He was hesitating. For a moment Beano was sure he was going to call a time-out to talk over the changed situation with his coach. That's what Beano would have done. But then the Carterville quarterback went ahead, leaning in and calling the signals.

Across the field, the Carterville coach was taking a step forward, as if to signal for a time-out—but it was too late.

Beano, recalling Marty's pass play with two yards to go for a first down, knew the frustrated feeling of the Carterville coach watching his quarterback make a mistake.

The quarterback took the snap, stepped back, and handed off to the fullback hitting inside guard.

The fullback almost made it to the line of scrimmage. Then he hit something and fell back in the clutches of two Barton High defenders. One of them was Larry Slider.

The referee put the ball down on the twenty-yard line, a loss of one yard, leaving the Bobcats facing second down and eleven yards to go for a first down, deep in their own territory.

From the Carterville bench, a substitute came running onto the field.

The Carterville coach was sending a message to the quarterback. Beano was sure he knew the contents of the message: Throw a pass, over and beyond the linebackers, into some of that empty space back there.

Beano shouted: "Larry!"

Larry looked at Beano.

Beano shifted his clipboard to his left hand and raised his right hand behind his ear, imitating a passer.

Larry was nodding even before Beano completed the gesture. Larry's guess was the same as Beano's. Larry said something to his teammates at linebacker and turned and said something to Barney and Billy in the secondary.

When the Carterville players broke the huddle and lined up, Beano looked at his three linebackers. They were playing a strange system, operating in unfamiliar positions. Was that good? Probably not, he told himself. But the Tigers had to stop the Carterville ground game somehow.

Beano realized his palms were sweaty. He'd wiped them on his jacket without thinking earlier. Now he wanted to wipe them again. But this time he didn't. How would that look at a crucial point in the game?

For one moment Beano wondered if Coach

Pritchard had, indeed, fallen off his hospital bed when Zip Logan described the three-linebacker formation. Coach Pritchard now would know that a pass into space in the secondary was coming. Coach Pritchard always seemed to know everything.

The quarterback took the snap. He stepped back. He extended the ball to the fullback slamming into the middle of the line.

Larry, at middle linebacker, stood his ground, waiting. Chickie and Clark, a yard wider than usual, waited.

Then the quarterback withdrew the ball from the fullback and rolled back to his right.

A Carterville halfback was moving out into the right flat, going wide.

Beano heard Larry's shout—"Pass!"

Chickie moved out with the Carterville halfback.

Beano wanted to close his eyes, cover them with his hands—he didn't want to watch.

Then the Carterville halfback broke into a sprint straight ahead, passing Chickie, who turned and gave chase. Barney Meddaugh began moving up.

The Carterville quarterback turned to his right and cocked his arm.

A couple of Barton High tacklers were breaking through the line, and Clark was now racing across from his linebacker position toward the quarterback.

The quarterback fired his pass a second or two before he wanted to and sent a wobbler floating downfield.

Beano stood with his clenched left fist in front of him, waiting.

The pass, hopelessly underthrown, fell to the ground, with Chickie and Barney and the Carterville halfback all making futile dives toward the ball.

Beano exhaled and turned and, this time, did wipe his damp palms on his jacket. Who cared how it looked?

Now everyone understood why the Carterville quarterback had not thrown a single pass in the first half. He had a slow release and a weak passing arm. The Carterville Bobcats concentrated on the ground game with good reason.

Another Carterville substitute ran onto the field. Another message from the coach? For sure, Beano thought. But what? He had no idea. He frowned. His lack of an answer was frightening. He looked across the field. His opposing coach was a real coach, not a student manager standing in. If this game came down to a battle of wits, strategy, and experience, Beano had no chance. No chance at all.

On the next play the quarterback stepped aside at the last second and the center snapped the ball back to the fullback, who punted.

The quick kick caught everyone, including Beano, by surprise. Barney Meddaugh and Billy Hale watched the kick sail over their heads. They turned and chased after it.

The kick was a good one, going forty yards in the air, and took a bad bounce for the Barton High Tigers.

Barney and Billy wound up circling the ball with three Carterville tacklers at the Barton High thirty-four-yard line.

Beano caught himself nodding his head unconsciously in admiration. Coach Prescott had called a smart play. At third down and eleven yards to go for a first down against a strange new defense, his Bobcats probably were going to have to kick on the next play anyway. Why not catch the Tigers by surprise? This way, the Carterville Bobcats gave away the ball in return for a lot of yards—and in return for a chance for the coach to discuss the new defense with his quarterback.

Beano decided he had wasted enough time

admiring the Carterville coach's move and headed down the sideline for a word with Marty before the offense took the field.

As he went, Beano glanced at the defensive unit coming off the field, and a sudden thought put a grin on his face. The third linebacker had, indeed, forced the Carterville Bobcats to give up the ball. The Barton High defense was coming off the field for some rest. And the Barton High offense was taking over.

Marty, with handoffs to Thurman, pitchouts to Todd, and two short passes to Art, marched the Tigers to two first downs and into Carterville territory.

Then Thurman was stopped for no gain over tackle and Todd lost two yards trying to circle left end.

Third down and twelve yards to go.

Marty, heading for the huddle, cast a defiant look at Beano. In all likelihood, he was expecting to see Beano pat Dave Harris on the back and send him running into the game for a long pass.

Beano, unmoving, returned Marty's gaze. It was a passing down, for sure, and Beano assumed that Marty knew it. But this was not the long-pass situation Beano envisioned for Dave.

Marty called the play, then lined up the team. The Carterville Bobcats knew a pass was coming. One of the linebackers was hanging back, ready to track any receiver cutting across behind the line of scrimmage.

Marty took the snap and backpedaled, bringing the ball up as he moved. Todd ran across the line of scrimmage and cut sharply, racing behind the line, about six yards deep, taking the linebacker with him. Art ran eight yards straight ahead and veered toward the sideline, looking back.

Marty fired the ball to Art.

A blitzing linebacker threw his hand in the air and tipped the pass, sending it ricocheting into the air. The ball came down in the hands of a white-jerseyed Carterville player. The Carterville player, a lineman, gawked in astonishment at the ball in his hands, and then started running.

There was nothing between the Carterville player and the goal except open space, and he ran untouched to the end zone.

Beano kicked the ground with the toe of his shoe and watched the scoreboard blink: Tigers 7, Visitors 6.

Then he ran down the sideline to meet Marty coming off the field. "Nobody's fault! Nobody's fault!" he called out. "We'll get 'em. We'll get 'em."

Carterville kicked good: 7–7, with the third quarter half gone.

While the teams lined up for Carterville to kick off to Todd, Beano stood at the sideline, clipboard in his right hand, and stared across the field at nothing for a moment.

Absently he lifted the clipboard and glanced down at the top sheet of paper. His eyes scanned the penciled words. The Tigers were on track with the game plan—except for Marty's stupid decision to try a long pass. The third linebacker was helping the defense against the Bobcats' powerful ground game. Marty's short passes had, as planned, worked against the blitzing linebackers in the early going, and the threat of the short passes was now making the linebackers hesitant with their blitzes. The ideas were working—but still, the Tigers stood no better right now than a 7–7 tie.

There had to be something in the game plan— some hint from the two coaches, something from Beano's imagination in there, in the jottings—that would shift the Tigers' offense into a higher gear.

Or maybe they were reaching the point where the planning had done its work and only the players on the field, each doing a job, could win the game.

Maybe.

Then the kick was in the air.

Beano lowered the clipboard in his right hand and watched Todd gather in the ball on the sixteen-yard line. Todd ran straight ahead, toward a crowd of Barton High blockers clustered in the center of the field. He banged his way forward to the thirty-two-yard line.

Thurman hit the line for three yards on the first play. Todd got five yards off tackle. Marty rolled left on an option, cut inside end, and gained three for a first down on the forty-three-yard line.

Okay so far.

Marty fired a short pass to Joe Burgess. Joe grabbed the ball, and the Carterville defensive half-back, moving up quickly, tackled him on the spot. The play gained five yards.

Beano blinked at the play. It wasn't the pass completion, nor the five-yard gain, that caused Beano to break out of his stance, drop his arms to his sides, and take an involuntary step forward.

The defensive halfback had tackled Joe by moving up quickly—too quickly, Beano thought—and he had been doing it the whole game. Beano had been watching him, but the implications of the defensive back's overeager charge hadn't registered before. Not until now.

If Joe ran a slightly different pattern, and the defensive back charged forward as usual, Joe could turn the defensive back all the way around and leave him behind, alone and confused. And if Marty got the ball to Joe, Joe was sure to score.

Beano's mind whirled. He thought of calling a time-out. But as Marty gave Beano a glance before leaning into the huddle, Beano decided against it. The play that Beano wanted did not exist in the Tigers' playbook. He needed to sell Marty and Joe on it. That could not be done in a time-out.

While Marty raced around right end for four yards, Beano stood at the sideline scribbling furiously with a pencil on a sheet of paper on the clipboard.

On the next play Todd, angling off tackle, fumbled, and the Bobcats recovered on the Barton High forty-five-yard line.

Beano dropped his left hand with the clipboard to his side and stomped the ground with his right foot. First a fluke of an interception and a Carterville touchdown. Now a fumble, turning the ball over to Carterville.

"It's okay," he called out to the dejected Todd, approaching the sidelines. "It's okay."

Marty was leaning down close into Beano's

face. "Beano, for crying out loud, will you cut out this master-strategist stuff and let us play the game?"

Beano was looking up at Marty, teeth clenched. "It'll work, and we're going to do it," he said.

"We've never even run the play in practice. What do you think this is—backyard football—drawing plays as we go? Next thing I know, you'll be—"

"It's exactly the same as the play in the play-book—except that Joe cuts right instead of running straight, and you throw to him in a different place."

"Beano—"

Beano turned from Marty and called out, "Joe, come here a minute."

On the field, the Carterville Bobcats, running left, then right—trying to avoid the slashing tackles of Larry Slider in the middle—were moving.

Beano watched the referee place the ball down on the Barton High twenty-nine-yard line and signal a first down. Then Beano turned to Joe.

Joe listened to Beano's explanation and looked at the scrawling on the top sheet on the clipboard. Joe frowned as he listened and then studied the play Beano had drawn.

Then Joe nodded. "Sure," he said. "It'll work."

"Good grief, Joe," Marty said. "You want to run a play that Beano dreamed up in the third quarter—a play that we've never even tried?"

Joe shrugged. "Beano's right about that defensive back," he said.

"Okay," Beano said. "That's settled."

As Beano turned away from the conversation with Marty and Joe on the sideline, a giant roar went up from the bleachers. Beano looked out at the play on the field. A Carterville fumble recovered by the Tigers? Another wobbly pass attempt, this time intercepted by the Tigers?

Beano saw neither of those good-news happenings.

He saw a white-jerseyed Carterville player running in the clear down the far sideline to the goal.

Carterville kicked good: Barton 7, Visitors 14, with time running out in the third quarter.

Chapter 18

When the teams were changing ends of the field for the start of the fourth quarter, Beano was standing at the sideline with Larry Slider. The big linebacker was still breathing heavily. His fierce play in the middle had neutralized the area, and his furious chases menaced Carterville ball carriers all over the field.

Marty and the Tigers' offensive unit were on the field with a second down and six yards to go on the Barton High thirty-nine-yard line.

Beano glanced at the scoreboard: Still Barton 7, Visitors 14.

The first Carterville touchdown had been sheer chance—a lucky stab in the air by a linebacker, and a lucky Carterville defender standing where the deflected ball came floating down. Those things happened.

But the second Carterville touchdown was

something else. The Bobcats earned it, and they got it. And, Beano reflected, they had done it while he wasn't watching. He was arguing with his quarterback about a new pass play. Maybe, Beano thought, if he had been watching he would have seen a problem, corrected it, and Carterville would not have scored.

Beano wondered how Coach Pritchard always juggled all the complexities of a football game—and seemed to be right with every decision.

Marty was under the center now, calling out the signals.

He took the snap, turned, and extended the ball to Todd, slanting off right tackle. It was the same play that ended with Todd's fumble earlier. This time, though, Todd hung on to the ball and gained five yards, leaving the Tigers with third down and one yard to go.

Beano nodded at Marty's glance heading into the huddle. They both knew Coach Pritchard's rule in this situation—either Thurman slamming into the center of the line, or Marty running a quarterback sneak.

They both knew too, Beano assumed, that Marty was going to follow Coach Pritchard's rule this time. No chancy pass down the field this time.

Marty ran the sneak, forcing himself ahead

three yards for a first down on the Barton High forty-seven-yard line.

This time, when Marty glanced at Beano on his way to the huddle, Beano did more than nod. He held up his clipboard in his left hand and jabbed the stack of papers with the forefinger of his right hand.

To any of the Carterville players who happened to be looking at Beano, the gesture indeed must have seemed strange. But to Marty, there was no mistaking the meaning. Beano's right forefinger was tapping the revised pass play he had drawn on the sideline. Marty clenched his teeth and glared at Beano—and shook his head.

Beano did not know whether Marty honestly thought the play would not work—thought the risk of an untried play too great—or simply rejected in knee-jerk fashion anything suggested by the acting coach.

But at this moment Beano did not care which of the feelings might be dictating Marty's protest. He stabbed the clipboard with his forefinger again and returned Marty's glare. He also tried—maybe mental telepathy works, who knows?—to silently remind Marty that the Tigers had another quarterback ready to enter the game.

Joe Burgess, watching Beano's pantomime on

the sideline, got the message and said something to Marty.

Marty glared at Joe and shook his head, but it seemed to Beano to be less of a rejection than an expression of disagreement.

Then Marty leaned into the huddle.

Beano watched a moment. Then he looked around for Dave. If Marty failed to run the play as directed, Dave was going into the game at quarterback. Beano spotted Dave standing down the sideline, and then turned back to the scene on the field.

Marty was taking a few seconds longer than usual in the huddle. Maybe that meant he was explaining a play that was new and untried. Or maybe it meant that he and Joe were arguing. Beano could not see Joe's face. But he saw Marty's mouth moving. Marty was doing the talking.

They broke the huddle and lined up.

Marty took the snap. He turned and extended the ball to Thurman crashing into the left side of the line. Then he withdrew the ball and rolled to his right.

Joe, to the right, ran forward three steps. Then he angled slightly to his left, to the inside. It was the usual pattern.

Beano stood frozen. Everything—every single thing—had to go right. If one thing went wrong, the play was a loser. If a Carterville tackler broke through and brought down Marty, the play was a loser. Or if a tackler crashed through and forced Marty to hurry his pass, the play was a loser. And, of course, if the defensive back, for once, stayed in his proper position, the play was a loser. And in the end, if Joe dropped the ball, the play was a loser.

The defensive back raced up, heading for a spot in Joe's path. He was overcharging again. Fine.

The Barton High line held as Marty, still moving back and to his right, cocked his arm.

Suddenly Joe cut back to his right, veering toward the sideline. He ran past the surprised defensive back, who whirled in place, trying to keep up with Joe's unexpected move. Now he was facing the wrong way, and Joe ran off and left him.

Marty lofted a floater over the confused defensive back, and Joe, all alone and six yards beyond the defender, pulled it in.

Joe dashed down the sideline to the end zone untouched.

The roar in the bleachers had started when the ball was in the air and Joe was in the open. The noise from the bleachers doubled in intensity when Joe gathered in the pass.

As Joe was crossing the goal, Beano leaped forward, his right fist and his left hand holding the clipboard both reaching toward the sky, and let out a shout.

Never, never, never—never had anything felt so good.

Beano's play had scored.

Beano raced down the sideline and met Marty coming off the field. Marty was grinning, but he shook his head at Beano. Maybe there was nothing else for Marty to do. Beano shot a fist in the air again, and then the two traded high fives.

Beano met the laughing Joe and grabbed him in a hug.

"Perfect! Perfect!" he shouted at him.

Randy Wolfe kicked good, tying the score at 14 all.

From the kickoff, the Carterville Bobcats began another of their inexorable marches—slamming into the left side of the line, then the right, then racing around one of the ends, then back into the line again.

The Bobcats did not try another pass. They were content with a three-yard gain here, a four-yard gain there, and a slow movement through one first down after another, down the field.

And the Bobcats were getting their gains, despite the three-linebacker configuration, because weariness was catching up with the Barton High defenders. The pounding ground game was taking an increasingly heavy toll as the contest wore on.

Beano was substituting more freely. He wanted the defensive players to have a moment of rest, to catch their breath. But on the small Barton High squad, Beano knew that every substitution was a big trade-off in strength and speed and ability. Was a fresh—but smaller, slower—player better than a quick and strong—but weary—one? Beano did not know where the balance lay.

Weariness in the defense was not the only growing problem. There was also the clock. The fourth quarter was ticking away. Every play on the field not only moved the Carterville Bobcats closer to the goal but also reduced the amount of time left for the Tigers to come back and score.

A three-yard gain off tackle gave the Bobcats a first down on the Barton High thirty-three-yard line.

For the first time Beano wondered if the Carterville kicker had the distance for a field-goal attempt.

Carterville could win without scoring a touchdown—17–14 on a field goal.

They had to be stopped—and now.

Beano sent the defensive unit first-stringers resting on the sidelines—three of them—back into the game, weary or not.

Twice Carterville hit the line for a total of five yards. Then the Bobcats, on a pitchout, sent a halfback cutting back off left tackle. Bud Holland dragged him down after a four-yard gain.

Fourth down and one to go on the twenty-four-yard line.

Beano watched. Surely the Bobcats' kicker could not deliver a field goal from that distance. He'd be kicking from seven yards back, it was another twenty-four yards to the goal, and an additional ten yards to the uprights—a total of forty-one yards.

The place kicker did not enter the game.

Instead, the Carterville quarterback broke the huddle and lined up the Bobcats in a tight formation. They were going into the line for the one needed yard on fourth down.

Beano thought, It comes down to this. It comes down to one play. If the Bobcats make the first down, they'll probably go on to score. A first down would give them a big lift. It would demoralize the tiring Barton High defenders. If the Bobcats make it, they probably will go on to score, and to win.

But if not, Beano thought, we've got a chance to score and win.

The fans in the bleachers seemed to be having the same thoughts. There wasn't a sound as the teams lined up. The fans, like Beano, waited in helpless silence.

The center snapped the ball. The quarterback turned and handed off to the fullback charging into the right side of the line. No quarterback sneak— not with Larry Slider waiting there in the middle. The fullback took the handoff and hit the line. He needed one yard—just three feet, only thirty-six inches.

Then the fullback stopped, and then he fell back.

Somebody, and Beano could not see who it was, had hit the fullback head-on and stopped him in his tracks.

The referee untangled the bodies on the ground and signaled the ball going over to the Tigers.

Beano let out a shriek, and then was drowned out by the roar of the noise rolling down out of the bleachers.

The weary Barton High defenders began trudging off the field.

Beano rushed down the sideline and caught

Marty pulling on his helmet and starting out onto the field. "After a couple of runs, if we're out of the hole, try Joe on his normal pattern," Beano said. "After what happened to the defensive back last time, he'll probably be hanging back."

Marty nodded.

"And," Beano continued with a smile, "If he's not hanging back, give 'em our new pass to Joe again."

Marty nodded again. No argument this time.

Beano ran back up the sideline in time to greet the defenders returning to the bench. He ran among them, slapping hands and clapping them on the shoulder pads and shouting, "You're great! You're great!"

On the field, Marty handed off to Thurman for five yards up the middle and pitched out to Todd running around left end for six more and a first down on the Barton High thirty-five-yard line.

Beano looked at the clock: six and a half minutes remaining.

"Plenty of time! Plenty of time!" he shouted. "We go! We go!"

Marty took the snap and rolled out to his right, watching Joe Burgess run his pattern. The Carterville defensive back had learned a lesson. He was approaching Joe cautiously. Marty threw to Joe before the defensive back got there. Joe pulled in the ball and the defensive back moved in and tackled him.

The gain was nine yards, to the Barton High forty-four-yard line.

Second down and one yard to go for a first down.

It was the perfect setting to spend a down on a gamble. A long pass, if it connected—great. If it failed, the Tigers still were at third down, with a chance to make the one yard for a first down.

Joe was barely out of the grasp of the defensive back and on his feet when Beano on the sideline turned, looking for Dave. He spotted him. "Dave!" he shouted, running toward him.

Dave was nodding and pulling on his helmet. He knew what second down and one yard to go meant.

"You go in there and throw it as far as you can, and tell Joe and Art to get downfield, and one of them catch it."

Dave nodded his head jerkily and ran onto the field, his right hand in the air, signaling his arrival to the referee.

Marty's mouth dropped open. He gave Beano an angry glare. Then he lowered his head and trotted off the field.

Dave's entry into the game provoked a buzzing sound from the bleachers behind Beano. Everyone was asking someone what was going on. Was Marty injured? If not, had Beano gone crazy?

Beano met Marty on the sideline. "It's second down and one yard to go," he said. "We can afford to waste one. Dave throws long very well. Maybe it'll work."

Marty said something that sounded like "Humph" and kept his gaze on the players on the field.

Across the field, the Carterville coach stood still as a statue, arms folded across his chest, watching the change. Maybe he thought Marty was hurt, and the substitution of a second-string quarterback was a lucky break for his team. Either way, he sent no messages onto the field, directed no shifts in his defense.

Beano felt like holding his breath.

Dave took the snap and, without spending time on a fake handoff into the line, backpedaled almost ten yards, bringing the ball up as he moved.

It was a pass, and the whole world knew it.

On the right, Joe dashed straight forward. On the left, Art sprinted straight ahead. Todd, coming out of the backfield, ran a crossing pattern in front of the defensive backs, forcing them to hesitate a moment. Thurman took up a position in front of Dave to block the first tackler through.

The Carterville linebackers dropped back to cover Todd, and the two defensive backs raced after Joe and Art.

In the line, bodies clashed in a furious struggle.

Beano clenched his teeth so tightly he could feel a jaw muscle jumping. His left fist was a knot. Could Dave do it? Both Joe and Art had defensive backs trailing them.

Dave did a nervous little dance and pump-faked twice. Then he hurled the ball.

Beano watched the ball, up in the arc lights, heading to the left, toward Art. He looked at Art. Art was a step and a half, maybe two steps, in front of his pursuer. He was looking back over his shoulder.

The pass was coming down now. It looked short to Beano. The defensive back was in full sprint behind Art.

Art, watching, slowed a bit and caught the ball on the Carterville twenty-five-yard line.

Aware of the defensive back thundering down on him, Art veered sharply to his right.

But the defensive back seemed to read Art's

mind, and he swerved to the right with him, catching Art and throwing him to the ground on the nineteen-yard line.

At the sideline Beano turned to Marty and said, "Okay, now go back in and win the game."

Chapter 19

Marty gave a little nod without looking at Beano and raced onto the field to replace Dave, pulling on his helmet as he went.

Dave, coming off the field, had both hands held high. To Beano's surprise, Marty veered toward Dave, and the two slapped hands as they passed.

Beano took a couple of steps onto the playing field, arms outstretched, and greeted Dave with a hug.

Then the two of them were swamped by a shouting crowd of gold-jerseyed Tigers, all jumping and pounding each other on the shoulder pads.

With some difficulty, Beano extricated himself from the mob of players and stepped down the sideline to watch Marty run the first play from the nineteen-yard line.

The Tigers were breaking the huddle and lining up. If Marty had looked to the sideline for Beano's nod going into the huddle, he had found Beano among the missing, lost in the swirl of players greeting Dave. But, Beano thought, no matter. Marty surely knows to keep the ball on the ground and punch it into the end zone.

In the bleachers the fans, brought to their feet by Dave's long pass to Art, were still standing, and a constant roar was pouring down onto the field. They seemed not only to sense victory in the making, but they were certain of it.

Beano was sure too. The Tigers were going to move the needed nineteen yards and cross the goal and win the game. It had to be. It simply *had* to be.

Beano looked at the scoreboard clock. A little under five minutes to go. Plenty of time.

"Don't fumble," Beano whispered.

On the field Marty was rolling to his right. Todd was running wide, looking back for a pitchout. But Marty tucked the ball away and cut sharply off tackle. He gained four yards to the fifteen-yard line.

When Marty glanced at Beano as he headed into the huddle, Beano gave more than a nod. He pumped his fist as Marty leaned into the huddle to call the next play.

Marty then ran left—same play, opposite side—and gained five yards to the ten-yard line.

Third down and one yard to go for a first down.

Marty took the snap and lunged straight ahead for two yards and a first down on the eight-yard line.

Beano glanced back at the clock, now stopped for the officials to move the chains for the first down. Just over three minutes left.

The fans in the bleachers were roaring a rhythmic "Go! Go! Go!"

Beano, his arms folded across his chest, the clipboard dangling from his left hand, stood at the sideline, smiling. It seemed that Marty had taken Beano's directive literally—"Go back in and win the game"—and was determined to do it all himself. Well, Beano thought, okay.

But on the next play Marty handed off to Todd over tackle. Todd crashed through for five yards to the three-yard line.

The roar from the bleachers grew louder "Go! Go!"

And then Marty gave the ball to Todd again, over the same spot in the line, and Todd slammed and twisted his way through into the end zone.

Beano, standing at the sideline, did not cheer, did not shout, did not raise his arms in triumph.

All along the sidelines behind Beano the players were shouting and leaping and shooting their fists in the air and slapping each other on the shoulder pads.

The bleachers were a shouting, stomping mass of people, all on their feet, screaming themselves hoarse.

In the end zone, Todd, trying to get to his feet, disappeared in a swarm of his teammates. Marty, standing back after handing off to Todd, remained apart for a moment. Then he rushed forward and joined the melee around Todd.

But Beano stood still, very still, his arms folded across his chest, and smiled at the scene.

After Randy Wolfe's kick made the score 21–14, there still was a kickoff to the Carterville Bobcats and almost two minutes to go.

Beano moved among the members of the kick-off team, saying, "We haven't won it yet, we haven't won it yet. The game's not over yet, not yet."

But it was, really.

Edwin Deere tackled the Bobcats' kickoff re-turner on the twenty-seven-yard line. And the des-perate Bobcats, knowing that two minutes was not enough for their plodding ground game to cover seventy-three yards to the goal, went to the air with a new quarterback. He was tall and skinny, and he threw hard. But the first pass missed the mark. And the second, a long throw down the middle of the field, overshot the receiver and fell into Billy Hale's hands on the fifty-yard line. Billy tucked the ball away, ran past the off-balance intended receiver, and scampered twenty yards down the sideline to the thirty-yard line.

Two plays later, both of them quarterback keepers with Marty hugging the ball with both hands, the game ended with the Tigers on the Carterville twenty-two-yard line.

At the buzzer, Beano watched the players leaping around and cheering on the field.

Almost to himself, but aloud, he said, "We did it."

Then he trotted across the field for the coaches' ritual handshake at the end of a game.

Coach Prescott was walking onto the field toward Beano, his players in the background slowly trooping away toward the visitors' dressing room.

Beano and the coach met in the center of the field.

Beano extended his hand and Coach Prescott took it. Beano wasn't sure what to say. He'd never heard what Coach Pritchard said to opposing coaches at the end of a game. So he said, "Good game." Then he thought that might sound like a put-down coming from the winner. But he didn't know what else to say, so he let it stand.

Beano tried to withdraw his hand to begin the run to the dressing room. But Coach Prescott held it.

"Young man, you did some brilliant things," Coach Prescott said.

Beano looked at him in surprise. Then he said, "Thanks."

Coach Prescott nodded his head at Beano and released his hand.

Beano nodded back, and turned and ran toward the open gate in the chain-link fence, where the last of the Barton High Tigers were moving through on their way to the dressing room.

Beano was the last member of the team to walk into the pandemonium of the dressing room. The room was hot and steamy, although nobody had turned on the showers yet. Nobody was even making the first move toward undressing. They were all busy shouting and cheering. Beano had never before heard such a roar in the Tigers' dressing room.

For a moment he stood alone inside the door, looking around and smiling.

He slipped out of his jacket and walked across and dropped it on the training table, along with his clipboard.

Then somebody tapped him on the shoulder. He turned.

"Congratulations," Principal Tyler said.

Beano shook hands with the principal.

Then Mr. Custer leaned around and shook Beano's hand. "Congratulations," he said, smiling broadly.

"Thanks."

Beyond the principal and the teacher, Beano saw his father and Jeremy standing in the doorway. His father nodded, and Jeremy gave a little wave. Beano waved back.

Suddenly Marty was standing in front of Beano. He waved a hand at the shouting players. As the noise fell off, Marty said, "Hold it a minute."

Beano blinked, and then waited.

Marty stared at the floor for a moment, seeming at a loss for words. The dressing room was silent. Beano watched Marty until he looked up.

Marty said, "Coach Pritchard sometimes presented the game ball to a player who was a major factor in winning a tough game."

Beano looked up at Marty towering over him.

The quarterback took a deep breath and continued. "The coach can't give the game ball to a player this time, because the players are giving the game ball to the coach."

Marty reached to his right, took a ball from Todd, and handed it to Beano. "We couldn't have won without you, Beano," he said. "And all of us know it."

Beano took the ball in both hands. He looked at the ball a moment. Then he looked at the faces around him. "I—I don't know what to say."

Edwin Deere piped up, "Beano Hatton speechless? I don't believe it."

Everyone laughed.